77420

Baker + Taylor   9/98 $16. / 1.

Her
Blue Straw
Hat

C. S. ADLER

Harcourt Brace & Company

San Diego   New York   London

Library of Congress Cataloging-in-Publication Data
Adler, C. S. (Carole S.)
Her blue straw hat/C. S. Adler.
p.   cm.
Summary: Having grown to accept and love her stepfather Ben,
twelve-year-old Rachel is dismayed when his spoiled daughter
joins the family on their beach vacation.
ISBN 0-15-201466-7
1. Stepfamilies—Fiction.   2. Beaches—Fiction.
3. Vacations—Fiction.]   I. Title.
PZ7.A26145Hh   1997
[Fic]—dc21   96-50124

Text set in Bembo
Designed by Lydia D'moch
First edition
F E D C B A
Printed in the United States of America

Thanks to Lyle Butts of Wellfleet,
who tried to correct my boating descriptions for this book.

For my friend Ruth Shapiro,
whose generous sharing of the richness of her life
has given me much joy and some good story ideas as well

Chapter 1

THE STATION WAGON WAS PACKED so full Rachel couldn't see out the rear window. She had her summer books on the backseat beside her and the big blue straw hat Ben had bought her last summer because it matched her eyes, or so he'd explained the extravagant purchase to her mother. MJ had been shocked. "Ben," she'd said, "there are straw hats in the supermarket for a quarter the price you paid. That's a major hat. And for the *beach?*"

"It suits Rachel. It just matches her eyes," he'd said.

It was because of the hat that Rachel had realized she loved her stepfather. Before then she had warily watched him become part of her mother's life. Warily because she'd been comfortable with the way things were and he'd smelled of change as strongly as seaweed smells of salt.

"Did you shut off the water?" MJ asked Ben as he turned on the engine.

"I did," he said. "And I canceled the mail and newspaper and notified the police." He chucked MJ's chin affectionately. "Everything on your checklist is done."

But MJ was biting her plump lower lip. "Maybe I'll just go through the kitchen again," she said and reached for the door handle.

"If we forgot anything, it won't fit in the car, anyway," Ben said. "Come on, love. Sand, sea, and sun await us. We're off."

"Wait!" MJ held up her hand like a traffic cop. In an instant she was back inside the little raised ranch house whose mortgage payments had been such a struggle for her to meet.

Ben looked over his shoulder at Rachel. "What do you bet she's double-checking that she didn't leave the stove on?"

"Or she wants to make sure the back door is locked."

They smiled at each other. MJ, worrier that she was, just had to make sure all the little boxes of life were filled in properly. Ben and Rachel let things happen. "She could be your daughter," Mother often said to Ben, and it wasn't a compliment.

In a minute MJ was back with a paper bag. "We had all that fruit in the bin. It would have rotted if we'd left it in the fridge the whole summer," she said with satisfaction as she slipped neatly onto the front seat again. "Now we can go."

Ben pulled out of the driveway and headed through their neighborhood of small suburban houses toward

Route 90 and the Mass Pike. Over her shoulder MJ said, "I told Ben we'd never get you started this early. You must be eager to get to the beach, Rachel."

"I am."

"Well, I'll bet you'll be even more eager when you hear this. Remember the phone rang when you were going to bed last night? . . . You want to tell her, Ben?"

"That's OK, honey, you go ahead."

"Well, it's *your* daughter," MJ argued with him.

"What phone call?" Rachel asked.

MJ's blond ponytail flipped out of view as she looked back at Rachel and said impatiently, "Oh, Rachel, the roof could fly off and you wouldn't notice it. Ben's ex-wife called. She was on the phone for an hour."

"I was upstairs in my room packing, Mother."

"Were you? Well, anyway, you're not going to be as bored this summer as you were last year, because—"

"I wasn't bored last year," Rachel put in quickly.

"Of course you were. You hardly did anything but sit and read, except for a little swimming."

"And I fished with Ben."

"Which you hated."

"No, I didn't."

"Rachel always brought a book along when we fished," Ben explained to her mother. "So long as she's got a book, she's happy."

"I *was* happy. I loved last summer," Rachel insisted, disturbed as always by her mother's inability to understand her.

"Good, fine. But anyway, this summer will be better. Tell her, Ben."

His kind gray-green eyes met Rachel's in the rearview mirror to watch for her reaction. "My other daughter's going to be with us for July and August."

"Your other daughter?" Rachel's heart sank.

"Tina, his own daughter," MJ explained. "Her mother's taking a massage course in California, so she's sending Tina to the Cape with us. We're going to detour by the Boston airport and pick her up. Isn't that nice?"

"It'll be nice for me, anyway," Ben said, when Rachel was slow to answer. "Tina's mother never lets Tina be with me for long. I've only visited with her for a few hours at a time when I flew out to Missouri or when I saw her at her grandmother's house in New York."

"I met Tina," Rachel said.

"You did?" Ben asked. "Oh yeah. When you met my mother at Christmas last year. But that was just for an hour."

"She was . . . lively," Rachel said. She had a clear image of the wiry girl's brown eyes rolling dramatically as she described the subway ride she and her mother had taken from the bus station. Tina had been performing for the adults, and only when she'd won their smiles had she glanced at Rachel, a sharp, unfriendly glance.

"Yeah, Tina's a character," Ben said indulgently.

The first part of the trip past the Schenectady airport was familiar. Rachel would have been reading by now if she hadn't been hit with the surprise change in summer plans. Instead she was recalling the long, sunny haze of last summer. Why didn't her mother remember that Rachel had told her how wonderful it had been? Rachel had lain on deck chairs reading, and slept with the sound of the waves sighing on the shore all night, curled her toes into the warm sand while she looked for beach treasures, and explored the piney trails through the dunes with Ben and her mother. She hadn't just read. They'd gone biking on the National Seashore trails and eaten nut-sweet steamers Ben had dug from the clam flats. Even fishing with Ben had been a treat because she enjoyed his genial company and the big smile he'd give her for no reason every so often.

"It'll be good for you to have someone your own age to do things with," MJ was saying. "Keep you from being lonely."

"I *wasn't* lonely." Now it was Rachel's turn to chew on her lower lip, one of the few habits she had in common with her mother.

"No, you were a good sport about it," Ben said. "Never complained even that week it rained. Remember that endless jigsaw puzzle that turned out to be missing pieces?"

Rachel took a deep breath. Was Ben buying into the myth that she'd been bored? The miracle about him had been not only that he understood her, but that he even seemed to like the placid person she was, to think it was fine that she read so much. He knew how it was for her to exchange her quiet self for the lives of adventuresome people. Nothing was more magical than that. Certainly not the TV and movies her mother relaxed with after a long day in the dental office where she cleaned people's teeth. Mom thought sitting around and reading so much was laziness. She liked to check off tasks from a list. "Done," she'd say with triumphant satisfaction as if she didn't realize that tomorrow would bring more tasks that needed doing.

"The only thing is, Rachel," her mother said after Ben paid their first toll and they continued into the endless greenery of Massachusetts, "you're going to have to share that nice front upstairs room with Tina. Unless you'd rather move into the little back room."

"They can take turns with the front bedroom, MJ, and they can flip for who gets it first," Ben said.

"No, Ben. Tina's your daughter and it's your cottage. Besides, Rachel had the front room last year. It's fair Tina should get it this summer."

"It's OK," Rachel said quickly. "I don't mind." She did, but she didn't want them to think she was a selfish only child. She'd always been careful to share even the things she loved best to avoid that label. It had been applied to her only once, by a baby-sitter, but she'd never forgotten it.

Mother was driving when they passed their usual turnoff onto 495 and drove on into Boston. Ben was talking about fishing and whether the striped bass would be around this summer. He still hadn't caught the big one he dreamed of. "Tina probably won't be able to sit still for fishing," Ben said wistfully.

Rachel could hear in his voice how much he was looking forward to spending this summer with his daughter. Of course he would be, Rachel told herself. Tina was his real daughter. His blood was in her veins. Rachel was only a tacked-on child.

She swallowed and did what she always did when something bothered her. She picked up a book, this time the life of a sea captain's daughter who traveled around the Cape of Good Hope on an ill-fated voyage with her father and got shipwrecked.

The next time Rachel looked up, the car was parked at a gas pump. Ben was filling the tank and her mother was suggesting they all use the bathroom. "We might be in a rush at the airport."

Rachel marked her page with a unicorn bookmark that her friend Marni had given her. She followed her mother's athletic stride and bobbing blond ponytail toward the ladies' room, noticing how large her shadow was in comparison to her mother's. Whereas MJ was slim and muscular from the running she did with Ben and from aerobics, Rachel was big. She wasn't fat, just large boned and fleshy. Ben said she'd make a fine Norse goddess, but Ben always said things that made her feel good and she knew better than to believe him.

"You're not enthused about Ben's daughter coming, are you?" her mother asked when they were washing their hands.

Rachel was surprised at MJ's perceptiveness. "How come her mother's willing to send her all of a sudden?"

"She told Ben she's tired of her life in Missouri and she needs him to take Tina off her hands while she's making changes. Ben is thrilled, Rachel."

"I know."

"What don't you like about her?"

"I didn't—we didn't—have much to talk about."

"Rachel, it'll be good for you to learn to get along with somebody different. You don't want to spend your life with your nose in a book."

"I get along with people, Mother."

"Do you? Then how come you never bring anybody home or have sleepovers or parties or do any of that stuff girls your age do?"

"I bring Marni home, and Kay before she moved away."

"Oh, Marni! She's as bad as you are."

Rachel let the remark slide by her. She was used to her mother's well-meant gibing at her to be somebody else. "Did *you* like Tina?" Rachel asked.

Her mother rolled her lower lip out, thinking. "I thought she was funny. Of course, that was just for one afternoon. I wasn't thinking about how she'd be to live with. She did seem to have kind of an attitude." MJ gave Rachel a worried look.

"It'll be all right, Mother," Rachel said. It always touched her when her mother got anxious and fretted. Before Ben came into their lives, Rachel had been the one to reassure MJ.

Rachel had a headache from reading in the car by the time they got to Logan Airport. MJ parked the car and commented happily on what a convenient spot she'd found. "Right near the baggage-claim area with fifteen minutes to spare. How's that for timing?"

Ben's eyes sparkled the way they had when he'd been Rachel's fifth-grade teacher and he'd introduced a new unit to the class. Because he expected the unit to be fun, his students had, too.

Rachel had told her mother that Mr. Rizzo was the best teacher she'd ever had, and MJ had repeated the compliment at the first parent-teacher conference. Somehow that had led to MJ and Ben meeting again, to run together.

Everyone who knew Ben had told Rachel how lucky she was when he and her mother got married.

"Tina's had it kind of rough," Ben said now to Rachel in the parking lot. "Her mother's a hard woman to live with."

"I'll be nice to her," Rachel promised.

"I know you will, honey. What I mean is, if she gets on your nerves at first, give her some slack before you get mad at her, OK?"

"I don't get mad easily," Rachel said, stiffening a little because it seemed that Ben was criticizing her, too.

"I'm just nervous," he said squeezing her shoulder. "It's a new experience for me to be Tina's dad. If I act goofy, you tell me, Rachel. OK?"

"You'll be fine," Rachel promised him, and she kissed his cheek and laid her head on his shoulder briefly.

The passengers had already deplaned by the time Ben and MJ and Rachel got to the security gate. It seemed the plane had come in early. Ben asked about Tina's flight and was directed to the baggage-claim area. They didn't see her at first in the mob of people picking up their suitcases from the baggage carousel.

Then a shrill voice yelled, "Daddy," and Tina pushed through the crowd, lugging a bulging flowered canvas suitcase that surely outweighed her.

"Where were you? I thought you must have got the day wrong or something," Tina said in an aggrieved tone of voice.

"Sorry, sweetheart. Your plane got in early. How was the trip?"

"Long." Tina looked over her shoulder. "Where did that Carlos get to now?"

"Carlos?"

"Didn't Mama tell you he was coming?" Tina asked. "Where's that flight attendant, anyhow? She was supposed to stay with us until you came. Oh, there they are. Carlos, over here!" Tina shrieked.

MJ and Ben exchanged looks of dismay as a lean boy with a headful of black ringlets, olive skin, and startling blue eyes approached them with obvious reluctance. With him was a stern-faced flight attendant. She made certain that Ben was Tina's father, then took off quickly, as if she were glad to be quit of her duty.

"Carlos is scared of flying," Tina babbled. "Isn't that amazing? And he's older than me. He turned thirteen last week. But we're both in the same class next fall. That's if we go back to my school."

"Why wouldn't you go back?" Ben asked, staring distractedly at Carlos.

"Oh, you know Mama. She's sick of Missouri. She wants to move to California as soon as she gets her certificate."

There was a silence that seemed to last too long. Rachel took a deep breath, afraid they might stand there in a loose circle transfixed in confusion forever. She smiled at Carlos, who saw the smile and ignored it. His ice blue eyes returned to Ben.

"So did Carlos travel with you, Tina?" MJ asked. "Are we supposed to drop him off somewhere or something?"

"Drop him off?" Tina laughed. "He's here for the summer, like me." She frowned at MJ and explained.

"Carlos is Antonio's son. Antonio and my mom are together now. So Carlos is gonna be my brother when Mama and him get married."

MJ shook her head as if this information were too much for her. She and Ben sought each other's eyes again, but neither of them said anything. *Not in front of the children, of course,* Rachel thought.

She was beginning to feel sorry for Carlos, whose face remained expressionless even as his agitation showed in his twitching lower lip. He was carrying a bag, too, holding it with both hands in front of him. Tina had dropped hers and Ben had picked it up. Now MJ reached for Carlos's bag.

"I'll carry that for you," she said.

"That's OK," Carlos murmured, not letting go of his duffel bag.

Ben laughed abruptly. "Your mother always did like to take me by surprise," he said. "Come on, kids. We've got a long drive to Wellfleet."

A few minutes later, Rachel found herself in the backseat of the car, stuffed between Tina and Carlos with Carlos's bag under her feet because it wouldn't fit anywhere else and her books on the floor under Tina's feet. Rachel's blue straw hat was on her head for lack of any other safe place for it. Tina raised an eyebrow at it, as if she thought it made Rachel look ridiculous. But she didn't say anything to Rachel. Instead she began chatting at her father about how she and Carlos had nearly missed the plane because their tickets had dropped out of her mother's handbag in the cab on the way to the airport. Carlos was silent, staring straight ahead. *No question about the big, sunny front bedroom now,* Rachel thought. She would have to share it with Tina because Carlos would need a room to himself.

"Are we going to stop anywhere and eat?" Tina said. "I am so hungry I could eat a whale. I didn't touch any of that rotten airline food. It was all dry or gooey. Yuck."

"There's no place much where we can stop until we get over the canal onto the Cape," Ben said.

"I have some crackers in my handbag," MJ offered.

"What kind?" Tina wanted to know.

Rachel looked out the window. The summer she'd been looking forward to had disappeared as fast as the city skyline they were leaving behind.

Chapter 2

TINA'S NARROW BODY was blocking the view of the bay out their bedroom window when Rachel opened her eyes the next morning. Unhappily she contemplated her new roommate whose slender legs wove together into a sinewy back, split by a long tassel of straight brown hair. There had been no question yesterday that she and Tina had to share a room. What had surprised Rachel was that as soon as they were alone in the airy front bedroom, Tina had announced resentfully that she hated sharing.

"So which half of the room do you want?" Tina had asked, eyeing Rachel with suspicion.

"I like being near the window," Rachel had admitted.

"Really? Well, so do I." Tina had waited.

Finally Rachel had said, "We could flip for it."

"You had it last year, didn't you?" Tina asked.

"Yes."

"Then I guess it's my turn."

Sly, Rachel had thought, feeling helpless. She'd never been able to deal with aggressive people. At Tina's direction, she had silently shifted her belongings to the door side of the room and the twin bed there.

"I hope you're not messy," Tina had said next. "I like things neat." She'd divided the dresser drawers between them, taking the top and middle for herself, and promptly unpacked her clothing into them.

Rachel had watched, feeling like an unwelcome guest, as if the room had somehow become Tina's by right.

This morning Rachel's suitcase still stood open on the floor with clothes tumbled out of it where she'd poked about for her sleep shirt and toilet kit. Neatness took more vigilance than she had in her. Her mother often complained that she was too lazy to put things back where they belonged, but it wasn't laziness so much as disinterest. Putting things away seemed pointless when they would soon need to be taken out again. There had been times when Rachel organized her possessions in a frenzied effort to please her mother, but it never took long for her belongings to fall back into the jumble that seemed their natural state.

Last summer her mother had nagged her about her untidiness so constantly that Ben had suggested that Rachel should be allowed to arrange things as she pleased behind the closed door of her bedroom. MJ had agreed and thereafter enforced neatness only in the rooms they all shared downstairs. That had worked fine. Both Rachel and MJ had been relieved of a source of discomfort.

Now, however, Rachel realized she was in for it again when Tina asked, "When are you going to put your stuff away?"

"After breakfast maybe," Rachel said.

"Somebody'll trip over that suitcase. It's right in the middle of the floor," Tina said.

Rachel got out of bed and moved the offending case next to the dresser.

"It would only take you a few minutes to stick the stuff in the drawers," Tina said primly.

"After breakfast," Rachel repeated. This girl had pushed her around enough already.

"Does your mother work?" Tina asked in a sudden change of direction.

"She's a dental hygienist."

"Did she lose her job?"

"No. She got the whole summer off because her boss is moving his office and taking a long vacation."

Tina eyed the suitcase and Rachel's cardboard box of miscellaneous items like her camera and writing paper and the piano keyboard that she might or might not get around to practicing on. "Your mother sure buys you a lot of stuff," Tina said.

"No, she doesn't."

"Well, don't worry. I can't borrow any of your clothes. You're too big."

Rachel flushed. No matter that her mother said she had a beautiful face; her big bones and broad frame seemed like an affliction.

"Will she make us breakfast?" Tina asked.

"My mother? No, Ben does the cooking. But usually

I just have cereal anyway." Rachel tensed in anticipation of more questions, but Tina had returned to staring out the window.

How would she manage to get along with this porcupine girl? Rachel asked herself. She'd always gotten along with people by letting them have their way, but she was afraid that wasn't going to work with someone as demanding as Tina.

Rachel strained to hear the waves and couldn't. Their rhythm had soothed her all last summer, except when there wasn't any wind and everything was still. A swim would feel good right now. Rachel was wondering if the tide was high enough when Tina said, without turning her head, "Let's go to the beach."

"What?"

"I said"—Tina turned around and flashed her brown eyes at Rachel—"I want to see what's doing on the beach."

"OK," Rachel said mildly. "I'll be right back," and she went to the bathroom.

The door to Carlos's bedroom was closed. She supposed he didn't need to be invited to join them. He could find his own way to the path over the dune easily enough.

Downstairs the smell of coffee hung in the air. Rachel found Ben in the kitchen reading yesterday's newspaper and snuggling the blue whale mug that she'd given him for his birthday to his chest.

"Morning," she said and hugged him and kissed his knuckle. "Tina and I are going to the beach."

"Fine," he said with an approving smile. "Come back soon and I'll make you pancakes."

"I don't eat breakfast," Tina announced from the doorway. "But you could save me a cup of coffee."

"Does your mother let you drink coffee?" Ben asked.

"She lets me do whatever I want," Tina said. "Her and me have an agreement. I don't give her trouble and she don't give me any back." Her face was pert with self-assurance.

"Is that so?" Ben said neutrally. "Sounds like a pretty grown-up arrangement."

"Well, I'm as smart and tough as any grown-up I know," Tina said.

"We'll see." Ben's amiable smile was still in place. As a teacher, he was used to dealing with difficult kids.

"You're not like I thought you'd be," Tina said to him.

"I'm not? What did you expect?"

"I don't know. My mom goes for a certain type of guy. Kind of fun and— You don't even *look* like the type she'd go for."

Rachel listened in disbelief. What was wrong with Tina? Ben was not only a great guy, he was good-looking. His face was broad and pleasant. And he was fair.... Sometimes people took Rachel as his daughter. "You look just like your father," they'd say and Rachel would be flattered. If it was a stranger she was never going to see again, she wouldn't correct the mistake, either.

"Am I different from last time you saw me?" Tina asked him coyly.

"Not very," he said. "You're still the image of your mother. Same eyes. Same manner."

Tina sniffed as if she suspected the comparison wasn't meant to be flattering. "Come on," she said to Rachel. "Let's go."

It was too early in the morning for the sun to have

warmed up the air, and too cool for swimming, whatever the tide, Rachel realized. She grabbed a sweater from a peg behind the door. "Won't you be chilly in just that T-shirt?" she asked Tina.

"I'm not planning to go for long, just to see what's there," Tina said.

Rachel led the way on the sand path through the sharp-edged spartina grass that grazed her knees. One of the great things about the little gray-shingled cottage Ben had inherited from an aunt was that it was just one dune back from the beach, so the bay was visible from the upstairs bedroom windows and Rachel could walk to the beach barefoot through soft tan yielding sand.

The tide was high. Rachel stopped at the edge of the still water and took a deep breath of salt air and seaweed. A fishing trawler marked the line far out where sea and sky divided. A border of fluffy clouds broke up the lower edge of blue and that was it. No birds, no people.

"Nothing," Tina said punctuating Rachel's observations.

"Isn't it beautiful?" Rachel asked in rapture.

"What's beautiful about it?" Tina asked. "I don't get it. People talk like going to the beach is so great. What's there to *do* here all summer?"

"You can go swimming and walk and read."

"I don't swim. I only walk if I have to, and I'd rather watch TV than read."

"There's a TV in the living room," Rachel said uncertainly.

"Fine. Peachy. *That's* why I flew halfway across the country. So I could watch TV here instead of in Warrensburg where my friends are?"

Rachel couldn't understand what Tina was so agitated about. Cautiously, she suggested, "Maybe Ben would send you back."

"No chance of that. My mom sold everything we owned. We had a big garage sale and she even sold my piggy bank and my old ballet costumes. After she gets her massage-course certificate, she and Antonio are going to find jobs someplace in California. Then they'll send for Carlos and me."

"Antonio is Carlos's father?"

"Yeah. I hope they get married. I like Antonio. He's cool and fun to be around. Not like Carlos. Carlos doesn't say *boo*. He's boring."

"Maybe you just don't know him well yet," Rachel suggested. Usually, she found, people got more interesting when she knew them better.

"The thing is, Antonio still has a wife back in Puerto Rico. Him and Carlos haven't been in the States very long. How they landed in Missouri is a hoot. They helped some guy fix his tire and the guy asked them where they were going and Antonio said, 'Anywhere,' so this nut drives him and Carlos all the way to Warrensburg. Isn't that a hoot?"

"Umm," Rachel said, not sure she saw much humor in the situation.

Tina kicked at the sand. "We might as well go back and let Ben make us pancakes," she said.

"I thought you don't eat breakfast."

"Well, right now I'm hungry and there's nothing doing here."

Silently Rachel led the way.

———

"Not bad," Tina told her father half an hour later. She had doused her pancakes in gobs of the real maple syrup that the rest of them used sparingly because it was expensive. One jug was supposed to do them for the summer. Ben hadn't said anything to Tina about conserving the syrup. He seemed to be treating her as if she were an honored guest. Unless he was as leery of crossing her as Rachel was.

Carlos appeared when Rachel was sprinkling her last pancake with powdered sugar to save the syrup.

"Sleep well?" Ben asked him.

"Yeah. I was tired. It's late, huh?"

"Not really," Ben said. "It's just past eight."

"I always get up early," Tina said.

Carlos was handsome, Rachel thought. His blue eyes were startling in his olive-skinned face. His features were fine and regular. And he wasn't demanding, like Tina. His eyes had taken in the pancakes, but he wasn't asking for any.

"Feel like some pancakes, Carlos?" Ben asked.

"Sure." The boy promptly sat down.

"Help yourself to juice," Ben said. "It's in the refrigerator."

"So what are we going to do today?" Tina asked Carlos.

He was caught with the plastic juice bottle in his hand, transfixed, it seemed, by her question. "I don't know," he said.

"What do you like to do, Carlos?" Ben asked.

"Play ball."

"Well, there's a basketball in the garage somewhere. There used to be a net up when I was a boy. I haven't seen that around anywhere." Ben began puzzling aloud. "There's a public basketball court near the pier in town, but that's a three-mile hike. You could borrow one of the bikes to get there if you want."

"I've got a baseball with me," Carlos said. "No bat, though."

"Seems like I should be able to locate a bat for you," Ben said. He nodded to himself. "How about it, girls? You like baseball?" He was looking at his daughter. He knew Rachel didn't like any sport except swimming.

"I can pitch OK," Tina said.

"Fine. Good. I'll locate a bat and meanwhile you kids can explore the beach."

"Morning, everybody." It was MJ. She smiled at them all sleepily, looking like a cute teenager with her blond hair tied back in its usual ponytail and her legs bare under a long white T-shirt. "Any coffee left for me?"

"I saved you a cup," Ben said. "How you feeling?"

"Not so good. I think I'll go back to bed after breakfast."

"What's the matter?" Rachel asked.

"Just a little nauseous."

"You pregnant?" Tina asked sharply.

MJ laughed. Then her blue eyes flicked guiltily to Rachel.

"You're not pregnant, Mom, are you?"

"Well, actually, I am a little." MJ laughed again. Ben chuckled as if she'd made a joke.

Rachel was jolted. She stared at her mother in dismay.

MJ looked back and said quickly, "I was waiting for a good time to tell you. But now that it's out we'll talk about it together. OK? Later?"

Rachel nodded, too stunned to speak.

"My mom gets sick to her stomach when she's pregnant," Tina said. "I'm never having kids. I hate throwing up."

"Your mother's pregnant?" Ben asked Tina in confusion.

"Not anymore she isn't. She had an abortion before we left Warrensburg."

The adults seemed taken aback.

Rachel swallowed on a dry tongue. She hadn't yet gotten used to the idea of spending her summer with a stepsister. Now it seemed she was going to spend the rest of her life with a half-brother or -sister. She'd been an only child for twelve years, the only child of a single mother. There had never been a father in her life, so she hadn't missed one.

MJ had gotten pregnant when she had finally started college in her twenties. "I didn't want to be a wife, but I did want you," she'd told Rachel more than once. And now it seemed her mother was wanting, or anyway having, yet another child. *We'll talk about it,* MJ had said. Yes, they could talk, but what could be done about it? Nothing. Rachel felt as helpless as if a gigantic wave had just crashed down on her.

"I'm going to the beach," Carlos said.

"I'll go, too," Rachel said. She needed to go where she could breathe.

 Chapter 3

"My brothers and me go to a beach like this in Puerto Rico," Carlos said when they were standing with their toes in the water. He and Rachel were the only vertical shapes visible between sea and sky except for a white sail way out on the bay.

"You have brothers?"

"Yeah, four. I'm the oldest."

"So you're just sort of visiting here in this country?"

"Puerto Rico is part of this country."

"Well, I mean, visiting here—you know." Rachel was too flustered to recall what the relationship was between Puerto Rico and the United States. "I mean, Puerto Rico is an island, isn't it?"

He nodded, letting her ignorance pass without further comment. "My father came here to look for work. He lost his job at the power station and there's nothing else he can do back home but fish."

"Oh. But how come *you* came? I mean, you're not old enough to look for work. I mean...I'm sorry. It's none of my business, but—" Rachel ran out of nerve and fell silent.

Carlos had a beautiful smile. It banished the old-man gravity of his face and turned him back into a boy. "Nothing stops your sister from asking questions that are none of her business."

"My sister? You mean Tina? She's not my sister." Except, Rachel realized, in a way she was. "I guess she's my stepsister because she's Ben's daughter and he married my mother. But—" The idea of Tina as a sister was disturbing.... And now Ben and MJ were going to have a baby together. Another step—no, that would be a *half*-brother or -sister. A cold fist clenched in Rachel's chest.

"You don't like it that your mother is having a baby?" Carlos asked, reading her mind—or more likely the expression on her face.

"I really don't know. I mean, it's a shock. It was just my mother and me for eleven years. I didn't even have a father until last year when Ben and my mother got married." And that relationship had been easy to get used to only because Ben was so special, Rachel thought.

Carlos shrugged. "Sometimes it's nice having brothers to play with. But it's a pain when they get in trouble and my mama blames me."

"Why should she blame you?"

Carlos selected a flat stone and skipped it expertly. It made six hops over the water before it sank. "I'm the oldest. I'm supposed to watch out for them. That's why she sent me to the States with my father, to keep him from getting in trouble."

"She wanted you to watch your *father*?" Rachel asked.

Carlos grinned. "My father gets excited and doesn't think ahead; he likes to have fun."

"And you don't?"

"I'm serious, like my mama," Carlos said.

"Hey, you guys! Ben found a bat," Tina yelled.

As she ran down the dune toward them, she twirled the old wooden baseball bat expertly. Her thin arms were apparently stronger than they looked. "Get your ball, Carlos. We can play on the road. There's no traffic," Tina said.

"But there's poison ivy on both sides of the road," Rachel said.

"We can play here," Carlos suggested.

"There's no room on this skinny little bit of sand," Tina said. But she looked around her in a puzzled way. The ribbon of beach she had seen before breakfast had broadened into a skirt of sand. "How did it get bigger so fast?" she asked.

"Don't you know about tides?" Carlos asked her.

"They don't have them in Missouri," Tina snapped.

"She's got an answer for everything, this girl," Carlos muttered. "You want to play ball with us, Rachel?"

"I can't," she said.

"Why not?" Carlos asked.

"I'm not good at it."

"You can catch," he said. "Anybody can catch. I'll get my ball and mitt." He strode back to the cottage.

"I guess he likes blonds," Tina said, eyeing Rachel narrowly.

"What?"

"He likes you. He won't barely talk to me. And he asked you to play ball with us. It's because you've got that innocent, baby-doll face. My mom says men'll fall for pretty every time. My mom and me, we're a different type."

Rachel didn't argue. If Tina thought she was pretty, fine, but Rachel didn't see it that way. She suspected Carlos just didn't like Tina—and neither did she, so far, whatever Tina's "type" was.

Carlos was back with his hard leather baseball before Rachel could figure out how to get out of being the catcher. He handed her a torn, shapeless mitt. "Just hold out your hand when the ball comes and it will drop in your glove," he said.

Meanwhile Tina was vigorously jabbing at the air with the bat, putting her narrow hips into practicing her swing.

Carlos went into slow, graceful motion, knee lifted, arm drawn back—and there came the ball in a straight pitch at Tina, who swung the bat and connected with a sharp crack. The ball went sailing high over Carlos's head out into the bay.

"I'll get it," Rachel said. She splashed through the shallow water in her shorts and T-shirt to where the ball had plopped down twenty feet from shore. There the moss green water came to her waist and she couldn't see the bottom. She began feeling with her bare feet for the ball, wary of crabs and sharp-edged rocks. Carlos, who was wearing bathing trunks and a T-shirt, joined her. "It's somewhere around here," Rachel said.

"It's my lucky ball," Carlos said. "I've got to find it."

"We will," Rachel promised him. "Anyway, it's so

heavy, it'll still be here when the tide goes all the way out. We'll see it then even if we don't find— Here it is." She bent, submerging the sleeves and front of her T-shirt to pick up the ball.

"Thanks," he said. As he accepted it, his eyes did touch her face as if he liked her, and she was pleased.

"I can't catch," she told him again. "I really can't. I'm terrible at ball games."

"That's OK," he said. "You can swim?"

"Sure."

"Good. I like to swim."

They returned to shore where Tina was poking a stick at a horseshoe crab as big as a soup-pot lid. "What's *this* ugly thing?" she asked.

"It's a kind of crab that goes back to the dinosaurs," Rachel said, "except it's still around and they're not."

"It's disgusting."

"It's an animal," Carlos said. "Animals aren't disgusting. Only people sometimes . . . Listen, Tina, don't hit the ball so hard or you'll make me lose it."

"I'm a really good hitter," Tina said.

"Yeah, well, then hit straight down the beach."

He pitched her a few more balls and ran and caught most of them himself before they landed. Rachel, who still had the glove, caught one that was bunted her way. "You see," he said. "You can do it."

Tina rolled her eyes in disgust and sent the next ball he pitched her flying out into the bay again. This time, when the joint search effort ended in their finding the ball, Carlos said, "If we don't swim soon, there won't be any water left in this bay."

Rachel laughed. "It does go out pretty fast."

He threw the ball toward shore where Tina waited and dove under, surfacing like a porpoise ten feet farther out. Rachel thought of going in for a bathing suit, but she was warm and still damp from her earlier dunking so she swam in her shorts and T-shirt. She did a leisurely crawl that she could keep up for a mile if she chose. It was the one physical activity that came naturally to her. Ben teased her that she liked swimming because she could do it lying down, and she thought there might be some truth in that.

"Hey, how far out are you guys going?" Tina yelled from shore.

"I'm swimming home to Puerto Rico," Carlos called back. He submerged and reappeared even farther out.

Ben didn't like it when Rachel got that far from shore. He'd told her that since she could be hit by a cramp at any time, she would be safest swimming parallel to shore and no farther out than where she could touch bottom.

Rachel headed straight out toward Carlos to tell him the rules, but he was fast and she couldn't get close enough to speak to him. Suddenly he submerged and he was down so long she got anxious. Then he popped up next to her.

"Boo," he said.

She told him they were too far out and was relieved when he followed her back in without argument.

Tina had left the beach by the time they came out. Carlos picked up his tattered glove and his ball, stranded where he'd thrown them amidst the drying straw and shells from the last high tide.

They sat down on the dry part of the sand to drip off for a while, but Rachel was uncomfortable. The sun was hot and she burned easily. "I think I'll go in and change my clothes," she said.

"You're getting red," he said. "Too much sun for you."

"Yeah, I forgot to bring my hat." She thought fondly of the blue straw hat. "To keep the fair Rachel fair," Ben had said and he'd kissed the reddened tip of her nose gently.

"I don't know why my father went with her mother," Carlos said. "Her mother is just like her."

Rachel couldn't come up with a response to that that didn't sound mean. "I think I'll go change," she repeated as if she hadn't heard him. And she left for the house.

She was on the stairs when she heard Ben talking to MJ in the kitchen. ". . . the nerve of that woman, to dump an extra child on us without so much as a by-your-leave. That's typical of the way she operates. But if she thinks she can walk all over me the way she did when we were married, she's in for a surprise," Ben was saying.

Rachel backed down the stairs and went to lean in the kitchen doorway. Her presence was duly noted with a nod from Ben as MJ told him, "Good for you, Ben. But I don't see how you can do anything when you don't even have a phone number to call."

"If I could just remember the name of that massage place she said she was going to study at . . ."

"Maybe Tina will know," MJ said.

"Right. I'll ask her," Ben said. "Then I can leave a message at the school asking her mother to call me collect. She's good at calling collect."

"And you'll tell her we're sending Carlos back?" MJ asked.

"Yeah, I guess."

"He's a nice kid," Rachel put in.

"Yeah," Ben said. "Too bad, huh? It's not his fault he was dumped on us. I hope it doesn't hurt his feelings if we ship him back."

"Listen," MJ said, "any boy whose father's irresponsible enough to dump him on strangers without even knowing what kind of people they are has already been desensitized. Don't worry about hurting Carlos's feelings."

"You'd have to drive him back to Boston, wouldn't you?" Rachel asked quickly. She knew how much Ben hated the two-and-a-half-hour drive through heavy traffic. "I mean, wouldn't it be easier just to let him stay?"

"Do you want him to stay, Rachel?" Ben asked.

"Kind of, I guess."

"Well, that puts it in a different light." He looked at MJ and said, "It wouldn't actually break us to keep them both, would it? I mean, how much can he eat?"

"Keep him for the whole summer?" MJ said. "Do you really want to play baby-sitter to your ex-wife's boyfriend's son? You know, you're letting her manipulate you again, Ben."

He put his hand over his mouth and sighed. "Yeah, I suppose."

"If I were you," MJ said, "I'd call her and tell her what I think of her tricks."

"Umm," he said without enthusiasm.

"How come you married Tina's mother if she's so bad?" Rachel asked.

"Rachel!" MJ chided.

"No, that's a fair question," Ben said. "Let's see. She

was lively. She was different. That tough attitude of hers tickled me—Tina has it, too. They're fighters...And my ex-wife had a rotten childhood."

He grinned at MJ, who had often accused him of being a soft touch for anybody who hadn't had the kind of idyllic childhood he'd enjoyed. MJ operated on the principle of taking care of herself and her child first and foremost. Charity began and ended at home as far as she was concerned.

"Was your ex-wife's childhood as rotten as the one she's giving Tina?" MJ asked.

"I don't know if Tina's having a bad childhood or not," Ben said carefully.

"You think that cast of boyfriends in her mother's life is easy on Tina?" MJ sounded incredulous.

"Tina seems very attached to her mother," Ben said. "It's hard to figure what makes a kid happy, MJ."

"No, it's not. A normal life with meals and school and birthday parties—that's basic. And from what you've told me, Tina doesn't even get that."

Ben shifted in his chair uncomfortably and frowned. "What do you think, Rachel?"

"I don't know," she said and added quickly, "I'm going up to change my clothes." The conversation was depressing her. She suddenly felt mean to have been so unsympathetic to Tina.

"You can tell by Tina's eating habits...," MJ was saying as Rachel left.

Birthday parties, Rachel thought, remembering the wonderful pink satin princess dress with the pink foil crown that she'd worn for her eighth-birthday party and played dress-up in for a year after. MJ had always done perfect birthday parties. Had Tina ever had a good one?

Upstairs Rachel found Tina lying on the bed near the window, her back to the door. "Hi," Rachel said. "I'm getting into my swimsuit and going back to the beach. You want to come?"

No answer. Tina didn't turn around. Rachel thought she might be sleeping. She tiptoed around the room, stripping off her still-damp shorts.

It was only when she had on her suit and was applying more sunscreen that she heard the sniffle. Was Tina crying? *Now, what am I supposed to do about that?* Rachel asked herself. Just because she'd had a good childhood didn't mean Tina could share hers, did it?

"Tina," she asked, "are you all right?" It didn't surprise her that Tina didn't answer at first. Rachel waited. If Tina needed comforting, the least Rachel could do was try. Uncertainly, she approached the bed and touched the girl's shoulder. "Can I do something for you?" Rachel asked.

"Yeah—leave me alone." Tina whipped around in bed so fast that Rachel stepped back. "I don't need any help from you."

Tina was as fierce as a fox in a trap, and Rachel knew better than to approach wild animals with teeth. She turned and left.

Chapter 4

RACHEL'S MOTHER WAS SITTING in the sunny living room piecing the log-cabin design quilt she'd started making last summer. Every bit of it was to be sewn by hand. MJ said quilting was the best therapy for her. She liked the precision of it and that the finished product would last, unlike her work on people's teeth.

"There you are," MJ said cheerfully. "Want to go for a walk, just you and me?"

Rachel hesitated. She didn't feel ready to be briefed on the change in her status as an only child just yet. "I was just going to read my book out on the deck," she said.

"You can read later." MJ put her sewing back in her basket and stood up. "Ben thinks getting a sibling at your age is going to shake you up. It won't, will it, Rachel?"

"I don't know." Rachel had the urge to run and hide, but she knew she couldn't escape, not once MJ had made up her mind to have their talk. When MJ wanted to talk, she expected Rachel to listen. Boldly, Rachel asked, "Why do you want another child at your age, Mother?"

"My age? Do you think I'm so old? Thirty-seven's not old, Rachel."

"Ben's forty."

"Right, and that's not old to be a father."

"OK. But why?" Rachel struggled against the tears building up behind her eyelids. "Is it that you want a child with Ben? I mean, one that you made together?" The tears rimmed her bottom lids ready to fall.

"You're mad at me, aren't you?" MJ asked.

"I'm not mad."

"Well, you sound mad. I thought you'd be glad to have a brother or sister."

Typical of her mother to think Rachel would feel the way MJ wanted her to feel. "If it wasn't an accident, you could have talked to me about it before you got pregnant," Rachel said. It surprised her to hear that she did sound angry because she didn't feel angry. She felt bewildered and a little lost, but not angry.

"Rachel, I don't need your permission to have a baby. I'm the one who's going to raise it."

"And Ben."

"Yes, Ben and me. It'll be our problem. You don't even have to get involved with this baby if you're going to be so negative about it."

Rachel hung her head. She swallowed and thought with longing of her book.

"Anyway," MJ said, "I'm only in my third month.

34

We didn't want to talk about it until we were sure that everything was OK." Her eyes widened and she sounded distressed as she asked, "You don't think Ben and I will love *you* any less because we're having another child, do you?"

It was exactly what she did think, Rachel realized now that her mother had put it into words. "I don't know," she said miserably. She swiped at her eyes with the back of her hand.

"And I didn't tell you sooner," MJ continued doggedly, "because I was embarrassed. Ben and I can't really afford another child...Come on, Rachel, get your hat and let's go for a walk so we can settle this."

Rachel sighed and gave in. "OK," she said. She plucked her blue straw hat from the rack and put it on. She had heard MJ boast that she and Rachel were very close, that they shared everything. But it was a selective kind of sharing, Rachel thought. MJ told her what she wanted her to know and how she should feel about it. If Rachel tried to explain how she really did feel, MJ accused her of being foolish or babyish, or lacking courage or something else. It was always some lack in Rachel that made her feel differently from how MJ wanted her to feel. Ben was the only adult who had ever had the patience to listen to Rachel without criticism. He was the only one who understood.

"Wait and I'll get my sneakers," MJ said. She was barefoot and wearing faded blue jeans and a pink T-shirt with an emblem of pins stuck above her left breast, leftovers from her quilting. She did look young enough to be having a baby.

As Rachel stood waiting for her mother to return with

her shoes, Tina appeared on the stairs. "What are you doing?" she asked Rachel.

"Going for a walk with my mother."

"Can I come, too?"

"Sure, Tina," MJ answered from the downstairs bedroom doorway. She signaled Rachel with a glance. Their talk would be put off to another time.

"So when is the baby due?" Tina asked. They'd just turned off the sand driveway onto the sand road and started down the hill to the path that Rachel and her mother usually took through the pitch pine and blueberry bushes. It went all the way to the marsh, and in blueberry season it was easy to collect a quart of berries on the walk.

"Early December supposedly," MJ said. "But I was weeks late with Rachel, so probably I'll be late again."

"Maybe it'll be a Christmas baby. I always wanted to be a Christmas baby," Tina said. "My birthday's January third. Blah. Nobody wants to celebrate then."

"Do you like babies, Tina?" MJ asked.

"Not especially. They cry too much and I hate bad smells."

"Oh," MJ said with a wry smile.

"I'm never going to have kids," Tina continued. Her eyes darted at them each in turn to emphasize her remark. "I'm going to be a career woman and make lots of money and spend it how I please. Maybe I'll go on TV and be an anchorwoman or something like that."

"Sounds like an ambitious goal," MJ said airily. "I wanted to be a flutist but my father thought I should do something more practical. He told me he'd pay for all the flute classes I wanted if I'd get my dental hygienist's license. He was a dentist."

"So was that a good deal?" Tina asked.

Rachel, who had already heard the story, listened for MJ's response with interest. "It might have been, but about when I got the license," MJ said, "my father divorced my mother and ran off with his receptionist, and that was the end of my flute studies. I had to go to work. Not that being a hygienist's such a bad job. It's gotten me through a lot of stuff."

"Men always do that, don't they?" Tina said.

"Do what?" MJ asked her.

"Promise you stuff and then don't do it."

"I wouldn't blame men so much as— Oh, I don't know," MJ said. "Life comes out in funny ways no matter what you do. You can only control it just so far and then it surprises you."

Rachel glanced at her mother with respect. She had thought that MJ believed herself to be always in control. It was one of the big differences between her and her mother. The only time Rachel felt in control of anything was when she was choosing a book to read.

They were walking single file now with Rachel in the lead on the narrow path between blueberry and poison-ivy bushes under the shade of the scrub oaks and pitch pines.

"So do you care if it's a boy or a girl?" Tina asked MJ.

"Nope," MJ said cheerfully. "Just so long as it's healthy."

"And are you going to stay home with it?" Tina asked.

"Now, there's the big question," MJ said.

Rachel was amazed. She would never have thought of the questions Tina was asking.

"I wanted to stay home when Rachel was born, at least until she went to kindergarten," MJ said, "but I couldn't. I had to leave her with a neighbor lady who took in kids, and sometimes when I picked her up she'd be dirty or scratched or hiding somewhere, but I couldn't afford anyplace better."

Rachel heard a regret in her mother's voice that amazed and touched her.

"This time around," MJ was saying, "Ben will share baby care with me if I want to work part-time. It will be hard, though, economically—I mean, if I don't work full-time."

"Well, Rachel can baby-sit for you after school, can't she?" Tina said. She eyed Rachel maliciously.

"Only if she's willing," MJ said.

There was a pause as if they were waiting for her to say something, but Rachel kept quiet. She didn't know how she'd feel about baby-sitting her own brother or sister. She didn't know much about babies. She'd never been near any. Once, when a neighbor asked if she'd sit for her little girl, Rachel had refused, more because she was afraid of being inadequate than because she didn't want to.

It was possible that she would hate this baby. Even now when the baby was just an idea, it made her sick to her stomach.

"Where does this path go to, anyway?" Tina asked. "I'm getting thirsty."

"We should have brought water," MJ said.

"It goes to the marsh," Rachel said.

"A marsh? You mean with mosquitoes and like that?"

"Sometimes you see interesting birds," Rachel said.

"Isn't there a town around here, or a store where we could buy some gum or a soda or something?"

"We're not walking toward town," MJ said. "And if we did, it would be a three-mile hike."

"It feels like we've walked three miles already," Tina complained.

"Only about a mile," MJ said. "Want to turn back now?"

"I don't like mosquitoes," Tina said. She turned on her heel. "I should have worn my sneakers."

"They're easier to walk in," MJ said. Tina had on flimsy sandals with narrow straps and thin soles.

They walked in silence for a while until MJ asked, "Tina, do you have a phone number where you can reach your mother if you need her?"

"No. She said she'd call me when she got settled somewhere."

"Well, do you know the name of the institute where she's taking her massage course?"

"Why?" Tina asked warily. "Why do you want to know?"

"Ben wants to speak to her."

"Well, he'll just have to wait until she calls," Tina said as if Ben were an intruder from whom she needed to defend her mother.

"How long have you known Carlos?" MJ asked.

"Just since my mom got his dad a dishwashing job where she was waitressing in Warrensburg."

"And when was that?" It seemed MJ was as good at asking questions as Tina, Rachel noted.

"I don't know. This spring sometime. But then I didn't meet Carlos right off. Not until they started going together, Mom and Antonio. He's a real cute guy, and he sings real good. That's mostly what they do together. He sings and she plays her guitar."

"You like Carlos's father?" MJ asked.

"Sure. Antonio knows how to laugh. Carlos is a sour-puss. And he doesn't like me. Well, I don't like him much either. I wish he'd go back to Puerto Rico like he's always trying to get his father to do. Carlos is a drag."

Tina was complaining about blisters by the time they were back on the sand road. She took off her sandals and hobbled along barefoot. MJ suggested she soak her feet in a pail of salt water. Rachel was hanging her hat back on its peg when her mother sent her off to the bay to fill a pail with water for Tina. The tide was so far out that Rachel had a quarter of a mile to walk across the mudflats to get water. When she turned to come back, there was Carlos.

"I'll carry that for you," he offered.

"We could carry it together," she suggested gratefully.

"Like Jack and Jill," he said with that transforming smile.

"Why don't you like her?" Rachel asked.

"She's a troublemaker," Carlos said with instant understanding of who Rachel meant. "You better be careful around her."

"Do you know how to reach your father, Carlos?"

"He said he'd call tonight. Probably he will."

She hoped that if his father called and Ben spoke to

him, they wouldn't agree to send Carlos away. She liked him. It occurred to her, as they squished back across the mudflats together, that she might have been lonely last summer without realizing it.

Tina was waiting for them on the front step of the cottage, barefoot and wearing Rachel's wide-brimmed blue straw hat.

Chapter 5

RACHEL WAS SO RARELY ANGRY that she didn't recognize the sensation that overwhelmed her as rage. "That's my hat!" she cried.

"Well, la-di-la," Tina mocked her. "What's eating you? This was hanging on a peg in the hall, so how was I supposed to know it was yours?"

"Ben gave it to me," Rachel said breathlessly. "Nobody wears it but me." To her surprise she was shaking.

"I guess nobody taught you about sharing, huh?" Tina said.

"It's *her* hat," Carlos said. "You should ask before you borrow something."

"Oh for heaven's sake. It's just a straw hat. There."

With a flick of her wrist, Tina sailed the hat off like a Frisbee.

The sand dune in front of the cottage was covered by a flourishing bank of poison ivy that Ben refused to kill. He claimed the ivy's long, deep roots kept the sand dune anchored in place. When her hat cartwheeled onto the ivy leaves, Rachel screamed and raised her hands to her cheeks.

Carlos went after the hat. "No!" Rachel shouted at him. "Don't touch that stuff."

Carlos stopped short and studied her as if she'd gone mad.

"It's poison ivy," Rachel explained. "I'll get some kind of stick to pull my hat out."

Carlos and Tina were still standing there when she returned with a rake. She leaned over the poison-ivy patch, careful not to come in contact with the gleaming green leaves, and lifted up the hat by the tines of the rake. Gingerly she dragged the hat toward her until she could pick it up by the crown which was the only part that hadn't come in contact with the oily poison exuded by the plants. "I'd better ask Ben if the hat's safe to touch," Rachel said.

"You mean poison could be on it?" Carlos asked.

"Oh, that's crazy!" Tina said. "And don't you go telling Ben I did it, because it wasn't my fault. How was I to know where that hat was going to land?" Defiant as she sounded, Tina's big brown eyes were anxious.

Rachel shrugged. With Tina and Carlos trailing her, she set off to find Ben. As usual he was fixing something, this time on his hands and knees with his head and shoulders hidden inside the doghouse-sized structure for the well pump. When Rachel called his name, he struggled back out of the pumphouse, coming up red faced and grease smudged with a wrench in his hand.

"My hat blew into the poison ivy," Rachel told him. "Do you think it's safe to wear anyway?"

Ben stood up and stretched his back with his hands on his hips. "No. I wouldn't take a chance," he said. "Give it to me and I'll clean it off for you." He took the hat by the crown, as Rachel was holding it, and walked off toward the house.

"You're not going to tell?" Tina asked.

Rachel shook her head. It wasn't in her to tell on people. "Just please don't borrow it again," she said.

Tina raised an eyebrow. "Sharing's hard when you're an only child," she said. "Believe me, I know. When my mother's friends' kids stayed with us and got into my things, it made me crazy." She showed her teeth and shivered her head to illustrate her craziness. Carlos laughed shortly and then looked embarrassed that he had.

"This hat is very special to me," Rachel explained, more because she wanted Carlos to understand than because of Tina. "You can borrow anything else I have, but not my hat."

"I can't use anything else," Tina said. "Like that patchwork wrap skirt in your suitcase? It went around me three times."

Rachel imagined Tina going through her belongings, foraging like a pack rat for what she could use. It was true Rachel didn't like the idea of sharing. No doubt that was a fault. But she hated the idea of Tina picking through her clothes.

"I'm going down to the beach," Carlos said. He took off without waiting to see if they wanted to go with him.

Tina watched him leave as if she couldn't care less. Then she turned to Rachel and said as if they'd suddenly become best friends, "There's a lot of hats in the cottage. Why don't we have a hat party? We could make cookies and drinks and invite all the kids you know around here to come. I went to a party like that once. It was *grrreat.*"

"That might be fun," Rachel said politely, "but I don't know any kids around here."

"None?" Tina sounded disbelieving.

"Well, I met a girl last August. She was visiting her grandmother at a cottage down the beach, but she was only here for a couple of weeks and I don't know if she's coming back this year."

Tina groaned and propped her sharp little chin on her two fists. "I could go crazy here with nothing to do."

Now it was Rachel's turn to be disbelieving. Nothing to do at the beach? "You don't have to *do* anything. Just being here is enough," Rachel said. She had daydreamed dreary winter days away imagining summer at the beach—the finger-length silver fish chasing each other at the water's edge, the graceful terns lilting through the air, the salt tang and seaweed musk, and the night sky so dark every star shone clear. How could Tina be Ben's daughter and not even like such things?

Rachel shook her head in disgust. "I'm going to read," she said and started toward the house.

By the time she began feeling hunger pangs, the heroine of her book had suffered through a storm and been left without shelter or food. Rachel put her book down and went to the kitchen. Ben was making dinner and Tina was helping him. "I'm doing the salad," she said importantly.

"Can I do anything to help?" Rachel asked Ben.

"You could set the table," he suggested. "I cleaned your hat with soap and water, and it came out OK, Rachel. It's on the peg in the hall."

"Thanks," Rachel said. She would have hugged him in gratitude, but because Tina was there, she didn't.

Instead she went to the windowed porch where they ate most of their meals surrounded by the small overgrown garden of flowering bushes behind the house. In the corner cupboard, there were just enough plates for the five of them but not enough matching salad bowls. Carefully Rachel folded sections of paper toweling into napkins. She heard Ben laughing heartily at something Tina had said. Even now, when she was outside it, Ben's laughter crept into the corners of Rachel's heart.

"...So then Mom told him she wasn't going to work there no more if he treated her like that," Tina was saying. "Mom told him she was a person, too, even if she didn't have a college degree. Nobody can make my mom take crap like that."

"I know," Ben replied, as if he did indeed.

Carlos appeared, looking freshly washed in a clean T-shirt and shorts. Immediately Tina asked what he'd been doing.

"Swimming," he said. "I got all the way down to the breakwater. Is it OK if I turn on the TV?" he asked Ben.

"Sure," Ben said.

Carlos went to the living room. Either he didn't like

their company or he preferred to be alone, Rachel thought. Tina didn't enjoy being alone. She had wanted to throw a hat party. Had Tina decided Rachel was OK because Rachel hadn't told on her to Ben? Possibly. But Tina wasn't a girl Rachel would choose for a friend. On the other hand, Ben would be pleased if she and Tina got along. What if tonight Rachel got out the cards and asked if anyone wanted to play casino or hearts? The five of them could play on the round dining table after the supper dishes were cleared away. Rachel liked the image of Ben and MJ and Tina and Carlos and her playing together under the halo of light, and maybe teasing each other and laughing.

Tina, it seemed, didn't want anything but pasta. MJ made her some noodles. "Plain," Tina said. "I just like them plain with a little butter. That's mostly all I ever eat for dinner."

"It's no wonder you're so thin," MJ said.

Ben didn't seem insulted that his stuffed codfish and home-fried potatoes were being slighted by his daughter. "Good, isn't it?" he asked the table at large.

"Delicious," MJ said.

"You seasoned it just right," Rachel told him.

Carlos said nothing, but he ate every bit of food put before him.

The phone rang while they were still at the table. Ben answered it.

"It's your father, Carlos. After you speak to him, don't hang up. I want to talk to him."

Carlos didn't take long. His conversation was in Spanish and consisted mostly of "*sí, sí.*" When he finally got his turn to talk, he gave what sounded to Rachel like a fervent plea with "Puerto Rico" the only words Rachel could recognize.

"What's he saying?" MJ asked Ben, who knew Spanish.

"He wants his father to go back to Puerto Rico and look for work there," Ben said.

"Carlos doesn't like the States," Tina said.

Carlos looked bleak when he returned to the table. Ben hurried to the phone and immediately began in his deep, carrying voice, "Well, it was quite a surprise when we picked up Tina to find Carlos with her. No one had mentioned that he was coming, too.

". . . Yes, well," Ben said, "it's true I'm a teacher, but this is my vacation away from kids. I hadn't planned to run a—

". . . No, it's not that he's been a problem. He's a nice kid, but this is a small cottage and one more person to feed and take care of is just—

". . . For how long? . . . But that could be quite a while, couldn't it?

". . . It's not a question of your repaying me. I mean, I'm sure he won't eat us out of house and home. But it's not something I agreed to beforehand and I resent being forced. I mean, I should have been consulted. *We* should have been consulted, my wife and I.

". . . Look, your telling him to do work for me isn't the point. Anyway, he's only a child and I don't want him to work." Ben's voice rose. "I just resent being taken advantage of. And I want you to understand. I'm not putting up with it for very long.

". . . Right. Oh, and before you hang up—I need a

number where I can reach you just in case...I understand that, but suppose something happens to Carlos?...Right. OK. Then we'll expect to hear from you every night about this time...Good. How about Tina's mother? Does she want to speak to Tina?...I see. OK, next time. Good luck finding work."

Ben came back to the table shaking his head. Then he saw Carlos's face which was a mask of utter dismay. "Listen, son, don't take this personally. We like you and you're welcome here. In fact, as of now, you're invited to stay as long as you like. It's your father and Tina's mother who— It's the principle of the thing. You understand?"

Carlos nodded, but he kept his head down and didn't say a word, even through the dessert, which was a tasty bread pudding MJ had made.

"So, any volunteers to do the dishes?" Ben asked when they were done.

Nobody said anything.

"The rule around here is whoever cooks doesn't have to do the cleanup," Ben persisted.

"I'll clear," Rachel said and she got up to start.

"I'll wash," Carlos muttered.

"I guess that leaves the drying to me," Tina said cheerfully.

When Rachel suggested cards after they were finished and the dishes were back in the cupboard, neither Tina nor Carlos seemed interested.

"I'd rather watch TV," Tina said.

"I'm going upstairs," Carlos said.

"He's still mad," Tina said when he'd left the room.

"About what Ben said to his father?" Rachel asked.

"I don't know. Carlos is touchy. I don't know if he's mad at his father or at Ben, but when he clams up like that, he's *mad.*" She imitated Carlos's expression so accurately that Rachel had to laugh.

"Mother, want to walk down to the breakwater and look at the sunset with me?" Rachel asked.

"Not tonight, Rachel. I'm kind of tired," MJ said.

"Being pregnant knocks you out, especially the first few months," Tina said.

MJ laughed. "You sound like an expert, Tina."

"Well, this spring the house we were sharing had three pregnant women in it, and one of them wasn't much older than me. Boy, was she sick! She cried all the time because they wanted her to give up her baby for adoption, but I don't know if she did. Her and her sister moved out before she gave birth."

"How sad," MJ said, and when Tina looked puzzled, MJ explained, "I mean, to be a child and have a child."

"Yeah, it's a drag," Tina said.

Rachel walked down to the beach to see the sunset. She had hoped Ben or Carlos would ask to join her, but neither of them did, and the sun plunked into its slot in the horizon like a great red dud of a coin with no afterglow.

While Tina and the adults watched TV, Rachel took her book up to bed with her. Next year, would she have to share this room with a baby? Probably the baby would be given Carlos's room. Unless they decided that it was too small and dark there at the back of the house and that a nursery should be full of sunshine. Then she'd be relegated to the back room. No doubt this baby wouldn't be too large or slow or lazy or quiet or clumsy like she was.

It might be clever and sly like Tina. And perhaps that was what MJ hoped for, a chance for a child more to her liking than the one she'd borne twelve years ago.

Rachel could remember how her mother used to come in her room at night and kiss her cheek or forehead. Sometimes Rachel had deliberately made herself stay awake for that kiss. Sometimes she had reached up and kissed her mother back. When had MJ stopped coming into her room at night? Rachel couldn't remember. She couldn't remember the last time they had kissed each other at all. The baby would need to be kissed. Well, babies were cute enough to be kissable, and even if MJ wasn't affectionate toward it, Ben would be.

Chapter 6

ON HER WAY DOWNSTAIRS to breakfast, Rachel saw
Carlos through the screen door. He was heading to the
beach with the fishing gear Ben had bought for her. She
was glad someone was making use of the rod and reel
because she felt guilty that she hadn't. Seeing a big fish
out of water gasping for breath had dismayed her so much
that she couldn't help rooting for it not to get hooked.
"Fishing" for her had meant sitting beside Ben with a
book to keep him company while he cast out his line and
reeled it in and cast it out in hopes that a live creature
swimming through the green vastness of the bay would
take his bait. His patient optimism had awed her and she'd
cheered his successes enthusiastically. Somehow she didn't
mind if *he* caught fish for their dinner, so long as she

didn't have to. And she was grateful that he never badgered her about her squeamishness.

"Where's Tina?" she asked her mother, who was alone in the kitchen.

"She went to town to run some errands with Ben."

"Oh. I wish someone had woken me up. I could have gone with them."

"Well, this was a good chance for them to be alone together, Rachel. Ben feels as if he doesn't know Tina very well."

"He said that?"

"He's told me that, yes. He feels bad that his wife never allowed him to be a good father. That's why he was glad that I had you when he met me." MJ smiled wanly at Rachel.

"You don't look so good," Rachel said.

"Morning sickness. It's a good thing I got the summer off. I'd hate to be working on people's teeth the way I feel."

Rachel made herself a bowl of cereal and sat at the counter to eat it.

"Do I look as old and awful as I feel?" MJ asked her.

"You look like a cheerleader," Rachel said honestly. Despite her paleness, MJ's skin was still creamy smooth and her slim figure didn't show any signs of pregnancy yet.

"I *think* that's a compliment," MJ said. "Thanks... So now that you've had time to get used to the idea, how do you feel about us having a baby? Do you think we're crazy?"

"No. It's just such a surprise. I mean, I've barely gotten used to Ben's living with us and now—"

MJ laughed. "Suddenly your family's expanding again. I know, but, Rachel, think about it from my point of view. You're almost a teenager. You won't want to hang out with us that much anymore. And in a few years you'll go away to college. You'll be leaving the nest."

"I will?" Rachel was amazed at herself. She hadn't even thought about leaving her mother and Ben. She liked her nest, and Ben's presence had only made it cozier.... It was disturbing to find they were expecting her to go away, imagining her separate from them. *I'm not ready to be separate!* she wanted to cry. Instead she said unsteadily, "I don't think I'll make a very good baby-sitter."

"Don't worry. We didn't factor that into our planning. But I bet you'll be crazy about the baby once it's here."

"Maybe." The conversation had made Rachel's chest ache. She was ashamed of the tears welling up in her and sure her mother would be disgusted by them. "I guess I'll go read," she said.

"Oh, don't, Rachel," MJ said. "Go outside and swim or take a bike ride. Sitting so much is bad for you."

"I've got big bones, Mother. I'm not fat."

"I never said you were, but you need to build muscle tone."

Rachel bit her lip. "Come for a walk on the beach with me then."

Her mother groaned. "What I feel like doing is lying down again."

"Maybe you should," Rachel said.

Instead MJ made a sudden break for the bathroom. Rachel could hear her gagging.

What if the pregnancy made her really sick? What if MJ *was* too old to have a baby? MJ had always managed everything so well. What would happen to them if she couldn't anymore? The house would fall apart. Their lives would fall apart.... No, they had Ben now. *He'll keep things together,* Rachel told herself. She took a deep breath and went to knock at the bathroom door.

"Are you all right, Mom? Can I get you anything?"

"I'm fine," MJ answered. "Just a little pregnant." Her weak laugh reassured Rachel.

Back upstairs, Rachel lay down on her bed and opened the book of Chinese fairy tales that she'd found in the hall bookcase, but her eyes blurred and she couldn't read. Supposing she didn't fit into the family anymore after the baby was born? *Go fly away, Rachel. You take up too much room here.*

Stupid, Rachel chided herself. *You're being stupid.* MJ would never kick her out. She was too conscientious a mother. She'd seen to it that Rachel had new clothes for the beginning of school every year and the same music and dance and swim lessons the other girls had. When Rachel wanted to invite a friend over, MJ always seemed glad and made sure they had cookies and pizza to offer the guest. And didn't her friends say they wished their moms were more like MJ? It was herself, Rachel knew. She was the problem. To be miserable because MJ and Ben were having a baby was rotten of her. She was a good-for-nothing kid who lay around reading all the time instead of doing things to make her mother's life easier. But just what was it she should do? With a sigh, Rachel sank into her book to get away from her thoughts.

Twenty pages later she heard Tina's shrill voice

downstairs saying with breathless enthusiasm, "Look what my daddy bought me! Isn't it the most you ever saw, MJ?"

"It's pretty, Tina, and that shape becomes you."

"That's what the lady in the shop said. I wanted to get one just like Rachel's in a different color, but the lady in the shop said my face was too small for that big brim. Don't you just love the flowers on this one?"

"Nice," MJ said.

Rachel closed her book. Now what? She went downstairs to see what Tina's "daddy" had bought her. Sure enough, Tina was showing off a straw hat with a circlet of flowers around its narrow brim.

"Look, Rachel. Like what I got?"

"Nice," Rachel said in an echo of her mother. Her dismay seemed mean to her, and yet there it was like an ugly spill on a new shirt. "Where is Ben?"

"He's putting in some part he bought for the pump."

Rachel turned on her heel and hurried to the backyard. Ben was halfway into the pumphouse on his knees. She could hear him grunting as he wrestled with the rusty piping. *Why did you ruin it?* she wanted to ask him, tell him, accuse him. But a few feet from him she stopped. She already knew the answer. Tina was his daughter and she, Rachel, was just his stepchild. Why shouldn't Rachel have a hat as good as hers? Better, because Tina was the real daughter.

For the dozenth time Rachel replayed the scene in the dress shop last summer, her favorite memory. She and Ben had been looking for a present for his sister's birthday and the saleslady had said, "Your daughter looks just like you. Such a pretty face."

"Thank you," Ben had said without correcting the saleslady about their relationship. "And believe it or not, this little girl's as good as she looks," he'd added.

Rachel had been admiring the hats, pretending not to hear the compliments; all the while they made her glow. On impulse she had put the blue hat on her head and turned toward Ben.

"It matches your eyes," he'd said. "You like it?"

"Sure. It's beautiful." She took it off and replaced it on the display holder. He went over and checked the price tag.

"You know what," he said. "A beautiful girl deserves a beautiful hat." She'd held her breath while he bought it, and tears had filled her eyes when he put it on her head.

"Oh, Ben," she'd said, "I love you."

They'd hugged each other right there in the store with the saleslady watching. "I love you, too, sweetheart," he'd said. He didn't often tell her he loved her, and she had never said it to him straight out like that before. The hat had put the seal on their relationship.

Without letting Ben know she was there, Rachel left him in the pumphouse and went back indoors. But she didn't feel like reading anymore. She laid out a hand of solitaire on the bridge table in the living room and played until the others were eating lunch.

"Rachel," MJ called.

"Coming," Rachel answered, but she kept on laying out the cards.

"Where's Carlos?" she heard Tina ask MJ at the table.

"Haven't seen him all morning," MJ said. "Do you suppose he's still fishing, Ben?"

"I'll go look for him," Rachel called from the living room.

"Carlos is OK. Fishing's his thing. In Puerto Rico that's what him and his father do all the time, he says," Tina reported. "Why don't you eat lunch, Rachel? After we're done, MJ's going to teach me how to quilt."

"I tried to teach Rachel last summer, but she didn't have the patience for it," MJ said.

"I wasn't any good at it," Rachel said stiffly remembering her clumsy fingers. "I'm going to see how Carlos is doing."

He wasn't in sight on the beach. She headed automatically toward the breakwater, a half a mile away, where Ben usually fished. Carlos was a lonely figure standing out on the last rock at the far end where the gawky channel light was fixed in concrete to guide boats into Wellfleet Harbor. Rachel stepped surely from one massive boulder to the next. She'd always loved walking on the multicolored granite riprap, picking her favorites by color. The pink rocks had been her choice last year. Now she was drawn to the more somber sage green ones.

"Catch anything?" she asked when she'd stopped a few feet behind him.

Carlos turned and fixed his blue eyes on her. "A guy gave me some of his bait. I got a few bites. Are bluefish good to eat?"

"Sure."

"That's what the guy mostly catches here. He said you have to wait until there's a run of them. In Puerto Rico I'd have had a bucket full of fish by now."

"Why don't you give up and come home for lunch?"

"No. I'm going to stay until I catch something." Stubbornly he turned back to his self-appointed task.

"Want me to bring you something to eat?"

"You don't have to. I'll catch a fish soon and then I'll come back."

"Carlos?" She sat down on the rock near him and wrapped her arms around her legs.

"What?"

"Do you like your brothers?"

"They're my brothers. I like them sometimes."

"Do you miss them?"

"Not much. Mostly they get into trouble and I'm supposed to watch them and I get blamed. I miss my brother Miguel, maybe. He's twelve. I'm thirteen, so we do everything together."

"I've never had a brother or sister. I never even wanted one."

"Yeah, and now you got Tina for a sister."

Rachel shook her head. "But she's not my sister. I mean, not really."

"Yes, she is. Don't worry, though. She won't be here forever, and then you'll be the only one again."

But she wouldn't be the only one again, Rachel thought. There would be the baby. "Carlos, do you think parents have just so much love, like a pie to divide among their kids?"

It was the kind of question most kids would duck by asking what she meant or saying they didn't know, but Carlos considered and answered seriously. "No, it doesn't get divided evenly. Some kids get a lot and some don't get any."

That was what she'd feared. She sighed. *Forget the hat,* she told herself. She couldn't compete for Ben's affection against his own daughter. As for the baby, she'd better get used to the idea that it was going to replace her. It would be small and cute and helpless, and it would have an absolute claim on MJ's affections.

Rachel stood up. "I'll go back and get you some lunch," she told Carlos, and without waiting for him to answer, she started the long hike back down the beach to the cottage.

"Carlos is still trying to catch a fish," she told them in the kitchen where, with the ease of dancers, the three of them were moving around each other to clear away what they'd eaten. "I guess I'll bring him a sandwich and eat mine with him."

"Good idea, Rachel," Ben said. "Tell him I'll take him out fishing in the boat later if he wants to help me get it in the water. Anyone else want to come?"

"I do," Rachel said.

"And me," Tina said. "I like boats."

"Really?" Ben asked. "You've done some boating?"

"My mom had a boyfriend that lived on a lake."

"Which one was that?" Ben asked.

"The bartender one last summer," Tina said coolly.

"Oh," Ben said. "Fine. Then we'll all go."

"Count me out," MJ said. "I'm still feeling queasy."

"You better wear your hat on the boat, Rachel," Tina said. "Your face is all red."

Rachel touched her hot cheeks. It was true she'd forgotten her blue straw hat in her rush to get to Carlos.

She put it on to bring him a cheese sandwich and one of bologna, a can of cola, and a peach. When he thanked her and stopped fishing long enough to eat, she told him about Ben's offer. "It's easier to catch fish from a boat," she said.

"I know, but I've got to do this by myself," he said.

He finished eating quickly without letting go of the rod. She was on the second half of her cheese sandwich when she heard him exclaim, "Yes!"

She stood up in time to see his rod bending as the fish ran with the line. "It's a big one," Carlos said bracing his body against the pull of the line.

He reeled in and let the fish take the line out, reeled in and let the fish go out again. It took a breathless fifteen minutes before the fish tired enough so that Carlos could bring it up onto the rocks with a last jerk of the rod. The blue had to weigh four or five pounds. It was big enough for the whole family to eat.

Rachel turned her back so she wouldn't see the fish suffer, but she said, "Watch out for the teeth. They're wicked."

"I see. I see!" Carlos said in excitement. "Can you find me a rock or something? I don't have anything to kill it."

She winced at the clattering and banging behind her as she ran off the breakwater down to the beach to look for a stone small enough to handle and heavy enough to do damage. By the time she returned with one, he had killed the fish with the metal bucket and was examining its teeth.

"We don't have this kind of fish in Puerto Rico," he said.

Carlos carried the blue back in the dented bucket with Rachel following behind him. "Here's dinner," he said proudly to Ben who was trying to teach a squealing Tina to swim in the bay in front of the house.

"Hey, that's a beauty," Ben said. He released Tina. She stood up in the shallow water looking wet and shivery.

"Want me to help you clean and fillet that blue, Carlos?" Ben asked.

The two went off to the side of the cottage where Ben had his fish stump still peppered with scales from the last fish he'd cleaned there.

Tina picked up the beach towel she'd dropped on the strip of sand up past the runner of dead brown reeds and seaweed from the last high tide. She wrapped herself in the towel and said, "I'll never learn to swim. Every time I take lessons, I sink."

"Ben's a good teacher," Rachel said.

"Yeah, he's nice," Tina said thoughtfully. "I don't know why my mom didn't stick with him. She always finds something bad about the guys she goes with after she's done with them, but she's never said anything bad about Ben."

"Maybe they just weren't compatible."

"What's that mean?"

"That they were just too different to get along."

"Yeah, could be. Probably she got bored. She gets bored easy. Anyway, it looks like he gets along good with MJ, right?"

"Yes, they love each other," Rachel said.

"You're lucky," Tina said. "My mom's too picky to get along with any guy. I'm picky, too. So I guess I'll end up just like her... Your nose is burnt. You don't tan at all, do you?"

"No. I just burn and peel," Rachel said.

"I tan easy," Tina said with pride.

Back in the cottage, Rachel disposed of the empty lunch bag. A jubilant Carlos was describing how he'd caught the bluefish which had yielded two thick grayish fillets.

"Eewww, that fish is a funny color. I wouldn't eat that," Tina said.

"That's why it's called bluefish," Ben said. "Don't worry. It turns white when it's cooked, and it tastes great. I'll grill it outside." He smiled at them all. "Now I need some help getting the boat in the water. How many volunteers do I have?"

MJ groaned.

"Not you, honey," Ben said.

"I'll help," Carlos said.

"Me, too," Rachel said.

"I guess so," Tina said.

"Off we go," Ben said exuberantly, and off he went with Tina and Carlos and Rachel trailing behind him.

Chapter 7

THE FOURTEEN-FOOT IMITATION Boston Whaler that Ben had bought secondhand last summer had to be hauled to the town's public launching ramp to get it in the water. Ben rolled up the door to the basement garage where the boat had been stored on its trailer over the winter. "There she is," he said proudly. "Our first job is to hitch up the boat trailer to my car." He fumbled with the latch on the trailer as if he weren't sure how it worked.

"You got to back the car up to it," Carlos said.

"I know. I know," Ben said. He got in the car which was in the driveway. Meanwhile Carlos quietly loaded the boat with life preservers, a gas can, and an anchor he found in the garage.

"How am I doing?" Ben asked out the driver's side window as he backed up.

Carlos, with some interference from Tina, directed him with hand signals, then locked the hitch in place.

"Good job," Ben said after he'd gotten out of the car to check. "You know about boats, huh?"

"A little," Carlos said. "You think maybe these tires on your trailer need some air?"

"Oh, right," Ben said. "We'll stop at the gas station on the way to the launching ramp." He patted the white fiberglass hull of the broad-beamed boat and said, "She's a good little vessel, don't you think?"

"Nice," Carlos said.

Ben grinned with satisfaction and directed them all to pile into the car. Carlos waited until the trailer and its cargo had cleared the narrow garage before he got in.

"I've got to sit in the front of the boat," Tina said. "Otherwise I get seasick."

"The bow's where you should be, anyway," Ben said, "since you're the lightest."

He whistled happily as he drove them out to the highway where he stopped at the gas station before turning right toward town, past the dory filled with petunias that separated Main from Commercial Street, and out to the marina. The launching ramp was near the harbormaster's house between the docks for the commercial fishing boats and the pleasure craft.

Tina spotted the soft-ice-cream stand at the head of the parking lot. "Boy, could I go for an ice-cream cone!" she said.

"Not right now, Tina," Ben said. "We've got to run this boat out of the harbor and all the way back to our own beach. I've got a mooring line for it there." He spoke to Carlos. "Had to dig halfway to China last fall to put it down where the winter storms wouldn't carry it away."

"How will you get your car back?" Carlos asked.

"One of the neighbors'll give me a ride back here later."

"I could run the boat back to the beach for you," Carlos said. "It's just follow the channel markers out of the harbor past the breakwater and to the left. No?"

Ben thought about it. "No," he said. "I'd better be in the boat in case it's cranky after its long winter rest."

"I'll *treat* to the ice cream," Tina said. "My mom gave me some spending money."

"It's not the money, Tina. It's the time," Ben said.

Tina rolled her eyes, but Rachel was pleased that Ben wasn't letting Tina push him around today.

Before floating the boat off its trailer at the foot of the ramp, Ben called a halt to the launching operation. "Time to put on the life preservers," he said and he handed each of them one.

"Why do I get this bulky orange thing?" Tina complained.

"It's the only child-sized one I have," Ben said. "You'd slide right out of an adult vest, Tina."

"I don't have to wear one. I'm not going to fall out of the boat," Tina said.

"Nobody goes out in the boat without a life vest," Ben said quietly.

"But why? I bet I don't even get wet."

"No doubt you won't, but the bay is tricky and you never can tell what might happen in a boat. You'll get used to the life vest. Just remember it's to keep you safe."

66

"Let me try the one you gave Carlos," she insisted.

Ben raised an eyebrow but he said, "Let her try it, please, Carlos."

Carlos undid the zipper and handed over his vest in silence. Tina zipped herself into it and said, "See, this is fine for me." It was too big on her, but Ben didn't say anything. In heavy silence Carlos took the orange cork-filled child's vest and put it on. It barely fit and he couldn't get the strings tied across his bony chest. His eyes went to Ben.

"Tina," Ben said slowly, reluctantly, "that really is too small on him. Listen, I'll get you a lighter vest as soon as I can, but for right now, it would be better if you'd make do with the orange one."

"Oh, all right," Tina said ungraciously. And the exchange of vests was made again.

Ben drove the car and trailer off the ramp. As soon as the boat was afloat, Carlos hopped in and tipped the engine back into the water. It had been humped over with its propeller up in the air. Rachel waded into the murky green water and heaved herself aboard. "Come on, Tina," she said.

"Am I gonna step on any yucky stuff in that water?" Tina's face was squinched up in distaste.

"Don't worry," Ben said as he walked back down the ramp toward them after parking the car in the lot. "I'll lift you into the boat."

He did easily and pointed her toward the narrow bow seat. Then he heaved himself clumsily into the stern, took the can Carlos had filled at the gas station, and fueled the engine. "We're in business," Ben said joyfully when it started on his first try.

"So what do you think of her, Carlos?" Ben asked over the roar of the engine.

"She's good."

"Yeah. She's got a thirty-horsepower engine and she's big enough for a whole family to fish from without getting their lines crossed. Besides, she's the first boat I ever owned." The boyish grin on Ben's face didn't diminish as he added, "Of course, she's a fair-weather craft basically. Wouldn't want to take her out if the waves were too high." He patted the outside of the hull affectionately. "We had some good times in her last summer, didn't we, Rachel?"

"Yes," she said and to please him she reminisced. "Sometimes we went all the way to Jeremy Point to fish and swim. The beach is great over there."

"So's the fishing," Ben said.

"Does MJ like the boat?" Tina asked. She was huddled into herself like a nervous cat, gripping the gunwales on both sides as they slowly followed the channel markers out of the inner harbor to the bigger body of water and their own beach.

"Oh, on a calm day, MJ likes boating. Any chop and she gets seasick," Ben said.

"It's choppy today, isn't it?" Tina asked anxiously.

Carlos gave the bay a contemptuous glance. "There's no waves," he said.

"Just a light chop out there," Ben said. "It should be fine, Tina."

"You ever stall out and have to row her in?" Carlos asked.

"She's too wide to row, and the current in the bay

can get pretty strong," Ben said. "But the engine's been reliable so far."

"You could fish all day in this boat," Carlos said.

"I do, Carlos," Ben said. "In fact, if you want, we could do that tomorrow."

"What about us?" Tina asked.

"You girls are welcome. As long as you promise not to get bored and want to come back too soon." He was looking at Tina as he spoke.

Tina eyed Rachel questioningly. "I bring a book along, usually," Rachel admitted.

"Rachel's not much of a fisherman. She has a tendency to root for the fish," Ben explained.

"She would," Tina said and she boasted, "I like catching them."

"OK," Ben said. "But today we'll just give you a little run around the harbor." He revved up the engine as they passed the rocks where Carlos had caught his bluefish.

There was a stiff breeze and three-foot-high waves once they got into deeper water. Ben increased their speed. Immediately Tina yelled, "You're banging my butt. Quit it."

Ben said, "Sorry," and revved up the engine even more so they skimmed over the wave tops more smoothly.

Tina screeched, "Slow down, will you?"

Ben frowned and patiently lowered the throttle. At a slow speed the boat rocked with the waves.

Tina promptly turned green. "I hate roller coasters," she said.

Carlos laughed. "Looks like you hate this boat," he told her.

"Well, if someone could just make it run smooth—"

"We'll be back on our own beach in just a few minutes, Tina," Ben said.

He angled the boat toward land and the spray hit Tina, who squealed in protest. The boat skipped determinedly from wave crest to wave crest. When Ben slowed it as they came into the shallows for a landing, the boat rocked wildly and water sloshed in.

"We're going to drown!" Tina cried.

"How can we? We've landed," Ben said.

Carlos jumped out and pulled them in the rest of the way.

"That kid thinks he's such a big man," Tina whispered to Rachel. "He was so proud of himself for catching that fish today—like it's going to pay his way for the summer or something."

"I like Carlos," Rachel said simply.

Tina huffed out a breath in disgust. "You would," she said.

"You're a good crewman, Carlos," Ben said when Carlos had the boat beached well enough that Tina could step out without getting wet. She stood there undoing the strings on her orange cork-filled life preserver as if it were soiled underwear she couldn't get off fast enough.

"Tomorrow could I run the boat a little?" Carlos asked Ben.

"Sure," Ben said.

"Well, I'm not going fishing if he's going to be captain," Tina said.

"Good, stay on shore," Carlos said.

Tina tilted her small nose into the air and marched off

toward the house, dropping her preserver on the sand for someone else to pick up.

"Looks like quilting's more her thing," Ben said calmly. "Want to practice running the boat around now, Carlos? This chop is about as rough as you want to be out in. Anything worse and she should be beached on the nearest shore."

For an hour Carlos practiced handling the boat without much direction from Ben. "Your father taught you well," Ben said.

"He wanted to be a fisherman, my father, but my mother made him get work on shore. Then he lost that job anyway." Carlos shrugged. "I won't be a fisherman, except if there's no jobs I can train for in Puerto Rico."

"Fishing's a tough life," Ben said. "And dangerous. I can see why your mother would want your father on shore."

Carlos nodded. He smiled at Rachel. "Will you drive the boat?"

"No, thanks," she said. But when they got close to shore, she was the one who hopped out to pull them in. "I think I'll go for a swim," she said.

She was stroking smoothly parallel to the shore in the heaving waves when Carlos appeared like a blue-eyed seal. He smiled and in silence they swam side-by-side nearly to the breakwater.

Swimming back against the current was hard, so they returned to the beach. They walked back along the shore past the squares and triangles of houses poking over the dune that separated the beach from the road like the rolled edge of a pie.

"Your father's a nice man," Carlos said.

"My stepfather," she said. "He's Tina's father."

"But she doesn't know him."

"Her mother wouldn't let her see him before this summer," Rachel said.

"Too bad for Tina. She'd be better off with her father. Her mother's a flake."

Rachel bit her lip. She hoped it didn't work out that Tina came to live with Ben forever.

"I like this place," Carlos said.

"Me, too," Rachel told him.

"It was a good day today."

"Because you caught that fish?"

Carlos grinned and didn't answer her. She took that as a yes. "Race you," he said.

But Rachel wasn't much of a runner. She ran a few steps after Carlos, then slowed to a walk, watching his heels kick up sand as he disappeared like a lithe brown sprite down the beach toward the cottage where Ben's boat tugged energetically at its mooring line.

Ben's suggestion that they all play cards together after dinner was immediately accepted by everyone. Rachel wondered whether they'd agreed to play tonight because he'd suggested it or because they just happened to be in the mood. No matter. She was glad to join in. They played Michigan rummy, a gambling game, using dried beans instead of money. It was a game Ben had taught to Rachel and MJ last summer. Carlos didn't know it, but he picked it up quickly. Tina had never played the game either, but she knew several similar poker and rummy games and was the big winner.

"I'm always lucky at cards," she said. "Paki, my mom's Las Vegas boyfriend, is a croupier and he says I'd make a good dealer. I'd like working in the casinos. And it's a good job, you know, because people always gamble even when they're broke."

"You think that's smart, Tina?" Ben asked. "To gamble when you don't have any money?"

"No, but people do it. So if they want to, why shouldn't I make a living off of it?"

"There's an ethical question here—," Ben began but MJ interrupted him.

"Why don't we just play cards, Ben?" she said meaningfully.

He gave her a rueful look. "Right," he said. "Leave the teaching for the classroom. So what do we give the winner? First use of the bathroom?"

"No way," MJ said. "I get the bathroom first because I need it most."

"I'd let you go first anyway," Tina said sweetly.

"Thanks, honey," MJ said.

Rachel wondered when Tina had become "honey" to her mother who seldom used terms of endearment. Probably it had been sometime in the course of the quilting instruction. Tina had a good start on a pink-and-purple pillow, which was more than Rachel had ever achieved.

On her way to bed, Rachel thought that the lively game of cards with the five of them sitting around the table in the orange glow from the overhead lamp had been as much fun as she'd imagined. Enough of a pleasure to compensate for not having her mother and Ben all to herself this summer? She didn't know how she felt about that yet. Still, she went to sleep feeling good about how the day had ended.

Chapter 8

THE INSTANT RACHEL OPENED her eyes the next
morning, Tina said, "I guess you're not going fishing
today."

"Raining?" Rachel yawned.

"It will be any minute. Look at that sky."

Rachel joined Tina at the window. The sky was
quilted with gray and white clouds. "You never know
around here," Rachel said. "It could turn out to be a nice
day, and anyway, Ben doesn't mind fishing in the rain."

"You mean he'd sit out there in an open boat in the
pouring rain to *fish*?" Tina asked. "Well, I'm not that
crazy."

"If it rains hard, I guess I won't go either," Rachel
said.

"We could play games," Tina said. "I saw you got Chinese checkers. I'm good at that."

Rachel's interest in Chinese checkers had waned after she was eight or nine. The game had come with the cottage when Ben inherited it, but all she said was, "We'll see what Ben wants to do."

Yesterday's T-shirt looked clean. So Rachel put it back on with jeans because the morning was cool.

"I never wear my shirts twice," Tina said, eyeing the shirt with distaste.

"It saves on the wash," Rachel said patiently. "The well's not very deep and we try to conserve water."

Tina raised her eyebrows and sniffed. "That's a good excuse."

Rachel flushed and had to resist an urge to yank off the shirt and put on a clean one.

"I couldn't sleep," Tina said. "That's why I got up so early. I'm worried that my mother hasn't called yet."

Tina's sudden mood switch surprised Rachel. The last thing she expected from this prickly girl was confidences. She remembered that Carlos's father hadn't called last night either. Ben hadn't remarked about that, but before he went to bed Carlos had said to Ben, "My father forgot to call. Sometimes he forgets." Then he'd disappeared up the stairs before Ben could make a comment.

"Do you think something's wrong?" Rachel asked Tina sympathetically.

"Probably not. Probably it's just 'out of sight, out of mind.' She figures I'm OK here so she's not worrying about me."

"Well, you are OK here," Rachel said.

Tina grimaced as if something hurt her and she said, "But she's such a nut. She'll do anything she feels like without thinking what could happen next. She needs me around to warn her... See, her and me have never been separated before."

"You must miss her a lot."

"Oh, I'm cool. I mean, I can take care of myself. She taught me that right off, before I even went to school."

"Anyway..." Rachel was still bent on being comforting. "Your mother's with Carlos's father. So probably everything's all right."

"You wanna bet? Just because Mom got him a job doesn't mean Antonio's in love with her or anything. He's using her to get around because she has the car and the knowhow. *Antonio* doesn't know beans about *anything*."

"She's probably fine, Tina. Don't worry." Rachel felt genuinely sorry. If it had been her mom who hadn't called, she would have been frantic even though MJ was a lot more reliable than Tina's mother sounded.

"I guess I don't really have to worry," Tina said. "I mean, my mom can take care of herself. She's a fighter."

"Like you."

"Yeah, we don't let anybody put one over on us." Tina's elfin face relaxed as if she felt better for having said that.

At breakfast, Ben left it up to his fishing companions. "The weather report says we might be in for some rain, but no thunderstorms. Do you guys want to go or put it off?"

"Fish bite good in the rain," Carlos said. "Let's go."

"I've got enough slickers for everybody," Ben said hopefully.

"Rachel's going to stay home with me," Tina said.

"I never said that." Rachel put down her spoonful of cereal and stared at Tina.

"But I thought— Oh, who cares. You guys go ahead and get wet. I'll keep MJ company."

"You can help me clean the house," MJ said with a smile. "That's my project for the day."

"I'll do that for you tomorrow, sweetie," Ben said.

"No, I'm in the mood to get the cobwebs out of this place. You go ahead and fish. I won't overdo, Ben. Don't worry."

Rachel made a picnic lunch—sandwiches, fruit, and a jug of lemonade—while Carlos and Ben went to load the boat. By the time she had the lunch ready, the sun was breaking through the clouds. *See,* she wanted to tell Tina, but there Tina was—obviously having changed her mind because she was already in her bathing suit— prancing over the dune after Carlos who was carrying a bucket and tackle box and life preservers.

In the entryway, Rachel set down the picnic cooler and searched the hat rack for Ben's old fishing hat. She couldn't wear her straw hat on the boat for fear of losing it. She blinked and looked again through the hats. Ben's fishing hat was there but where was her wide-brimmed blue straw?

She went back upstairs and checked out the bedroom, even looking in the closet although she knew she hadn't put it there.

Rachel got to the beach with the picnic jug and cooler, wearing Ben's hat and an oversized T-shirt over her bathing suit.

"I'm going with you guys after all," Tina said to her.

"Do you know where my blue hat is, Tina?" Rachel asked.

"Me? How would I know? You told me not to touch it."

"Well, it's gone."

"It's probably around somewhere. Maybe your mother borrowed it."

"My mother wouldn't—" Something about Tina's too-innocent face made Rachel suspicious. "Where did you hide it?" she asked Tina.

"Are you accusing me of something?" Tina's slight body stiffened and her back arched like an angry cat's.

"Yes, I am."

Roll of the eyes, hand on hip. "Well, if that doesn't beat all. You have some nerve accusing me just because you can't find your hat."

"I hung it on the peg and it's gone."

"Hey, girls. Don't squabble. Come on. If you're going fishing with us, let's go," Ben said.

In silence Rachel set the heavy cooler down in the boat and then the jug. She put on her life jacket. What could she say to Tina? She knew the girl had done something with her hat—to tease her maybe, or to be mean—but she couldn't prove it. What she would do was not talk to her, Rachel decided.

Ben had said that the reason weather was such a big topic of conversation on the Cape was that it changed more rapidly and more often there than anywhere else. On the bay that day, there seemed to be at least a couple of weather systems operating at the same time. The sky was a gray lid to the north and sunny overhead. Out a ways, the water was dark and rippled by the passing wind. But near shore as they started out, the water was so calm that even Tina, again wearing the hateful orange cork life vest, wasn't complaining.

She was telling Ben about a circus performer, another boyfriend of her mother's, who had tried to teach Tina to hang from her knees on a trapeze as high as a telephone pole. "And he didn't use a safety net either," Tina was saying.

The engine purred quietly enough that her shrill voice carried over it easily. Carlos was staring out at the fingernail-sized fishing boats gathered around Jeremy Point. That distant strip of sand that formed the barrier between outer harbor and bay was barely visible. When Tina slowed down for a bit, Ben explained to Carlos that Jeremy Point was the end of a barrier reef that protected the harbor waters they were crossing from the rougher water of the wide-open bay on the other side.

Suddenly Rachel heard a voice calling, "Ben! Ben!" She looked back and saw a tiny figure on the beach. It was her mother and she was using Ben's bullhorn to reach them. "Ben," Rachel said, "Mom's calling you."

He cut the engine and turned around. "Something must be wrong," he said when the call came more clearly. "We better go back."

Carlos's face remained impassive without a sign of his disappointment. Tina brightened as they headed back to shore. Rachel wondered why her mother needed Ben, but she knew she'd find out in a few minutes, so she returned to brooding about how she was going to get Tina to tell her what she'd done with her blue straw hat.

"You better take me to the doctor," MJ told Ben quietly when he cut the engine to glide onto shore. "I seem to be bleeding."

"You take over, Carlos," Ben said, and he jumped out of the boat and rushed to his wife.

Rachel stared at her mother in shock. MJ never had anything wrong with her. She'd never even had a cold bad enough to stay home from work for. What did it mean that she was bleeding?

Chapter 9

"MOTHER, WHERE ARE YOU HURT?" Rachel asked. She couldn't see any sign of injury.

MJ looked embarrassed and her eyes went to Carlos. "Oh, Rachel," she said. "It's, you know, the pregnancy."

"Oh," Rachel said, and now she was embarrassed for not having understood.

"Let's go, honey," Ben said. He took his wife's arm. Then he asked, "Shall I carry you to the car?"

"No, don't be silly," MJ said firmly. Her eyes took in the children facing her on the beach. "Ben," she said, "we can't just leave them here alone."

"They'll be fine. Carlos can handle the boat. Right, Carlos?" Ben asked over his shoulder.

"Sure," Carlos said.

"You kids fish for a little and then beach the boat and

stay on shore," Ben said. "I've got to get MJ to the doctor, and I don't know how long we'll be gone."

"No problem," Tina said.

"We'll be fine, Mom. Get to the doctor," Rachel said. It scared her to see MJ so white faced and thin lipped as if she were holding in pain or fear or both. Did "bleeding" mean she would she lose the baby? Rachel didn't know what to think about that.

"Don't fish too far from shore now," Ben said hastily over his shoulder as he ushered his wife off the beach. "Carlos is captain. Listen to him."

"Don't get your hopes up, Rachel," Tina said when they'd disappeared over the dune. "My mother's friend bled for months and had the baby anyway. It's no big deal."

Rachel shuddered. "I just don't want anything to happen to my mother."

"I told you, it's no big deal. The doctor'll just say she should rest. My mother's friend had to lie with her feet up for four months and she lost her job. Boy, was her husband mad because they couldn't make the payments on their car and it got repossessed. But the baby came out fine."

Tina's assurance was comforting despite her insinuation that Rachel didn't want MJ to have the baby.

"Anyway, now we don't have to fish," Tina said.

"You're the only one doesn't want to," Carlos said.

They both looked at Rachel. She glanced at the bay and said, "The water's so calm today, Tina. We could give Carlos a chance to fish from the boat for a while at least."

"We could run the boat over to Jeremy Point and you could fool around on the beach while I fish," Carlos said to Tina.

"I don't think that's the shore Ben meant for us to stay close to," Rachel said. "It's farther away than you think. It'd take at least half an hour to get across this harbor, Carlos."

"But he said we were going to fish there," Carlos said stubbornly.

"My father said Carlos was captain," Tina put in slyly.

The "my father" reminder stung Rachel. "OK. Fine," she said. "Let's go then."

Carlos did handle the boat as if he knew what he was doing. Their wake across the harbor made a perfectly straight line, and he inspired confidence by the way he stood with feet braced and hand steady on the tiller. When Tina complained that he was going too fast, he ignored her.

Rachel trailed her fingers in the cool gray water. She wondered how her mother was doing. The missing hat seemed like a minor problem by comparison. Before long though, her imagination failed her as to what could be happening at the doctor's office. Her mind wound back to the question of how to get Tina to return her hat. Unless Tina had already destroyed it!

Ben's daughter was so unlike anyone Rachel had ever known that she hadn't a clue as to how to deal with her. Be nice to her? Soften her up with kindness? But Tina would know what she was after if she tried that. What if she offered Tina a bribe? She could tell Tina she could have anything she wanted in exchange for the hat. Except there wasn't anything Rachel owned that Tina would want. Certainly not clothes. Tina had made it clear they were all too big.

Jewelry. Surely Tina liked jewelry, but Rachel didn't have much. There was a pin with pearls and diamonds from her grandmother. But it was the only thing Rachel had from her grandmother, and it was so old-fashioned Tina might not even like it. What about the silver necklace with the cat pendant Ben had given her for her birthday? She loved it, but Tina might like it, too, and the necklace was just a regular gift, not something with extra-special meaning like the hat.

What if she offered to buy something for Tina? Tina was wearing one tiny gold hoop in one pierced ear and nothing in the other. Probably she'd lost a hoop. Start with that offer and then go up to the necklace. Rachel hadn't worn it, except once when they went out to dinner. She'd imagined she might use it to dress up for a dance someday, if any boy ever asked her. Considering that boys seemed to like petite girls, or anyhow slender ones, it wasn't likely she'd be asked soon. Yes, if Tina wanted the silver necklace, Rachel could live without it. As for Ben, he'd probably think it was nice that she had given his gift to Tina.

The steady buzz of the engine was making Rachel sleepy. She looked across at Tina, who was stretched out on her stomach on the red boat cushions, chipping the pink polish off her stubby fingernails. What was Tina thinking about? Her mother maybe. That she hadn't called. It would scare Rachel to live with a person as unpredictable as Tina's mother seemed to be, but Tina sounded as if she really loved her mother. Probably a kid loved his or her mother no matter what, just because that was who the baby, the toddler, the child clung to. But Marni, Rachel's stringbean friend, had claimed to hate her mother. "She's a slob," Marni had said. "And she keeps telling me how much she loves me until I'm sick to my stomach." That had struck Rachel as strange because the one thing she found attractive about Marni's mother was her affectionateness. She even spoke lovingly to Rachel, whom she rarely saw because Marni preferred going to Rachel's house.

Rachel guessed that Tina hadn't liked being dumped on a father she didn't know. But Ben was so good. By now Tina must realize how lucky she was to have him for a father. Rachel would appreciate him, all right, if he were her father—not just a stepfather but a real one who would love her no matter what because she was his.

Clouds cast a shadow on the water. Rachel sighed.

Carlos remained standing straight backed and still in his baggy swim shorts with his hand on the tiller. He could have steered the boat sitting down, the way Ben did, but Rachel didn't suggest that to him. Carlos was too much in charge here on the water, as if it was his element. His shiny ringlets were flattened slightly in the breeze made by the boat's forward thrust. Was his curly hair soft or coarse? It looked soft. And his face was so grave and handsome. She bet she knew what *he* wanted. To get back to Puerto Rico with his father as soon as possible. Carlos must be upset that his father hadn't called last night as he'd promised Ben he would.

MJ could always be depended on, Rachel thought. Always. Suddenly she felt an immense gratitude for that.

There were no small gas-powered boats besides theirs

out in the harbor today, and only one sailboat. The water glittered where a shaft of sun hit it. Far out on the other side of Great Island, tines of rain were biting into the bay from blue-black storm clouds. Strange weather. And strange, too, how Carlos and Tina and she were each disturbed about something instead of enjoying this boat ride.

About ten feet from the beach, Carlos cut the engine. "OK, we're close enough," he said. The bay was deeper near this shore; it dropped off more sharply than on the populated side. But here the water was as transparent as in a drinking glass. Rachel could see a crab scuttling over the colorful pebbles on the bottom which had to be fifteen feet down. And there were shells, lots of striped orange and white or gray or brown scallop shells among the stones.

"Do you like shells, Tina?" Rachel asked.

"Sure."

"This is a good place for them."

"Anyone who doesn't want to fish can get out here," Carlos said.

"If you want me to get out, you better take us up on the sand," Tina said. She seemed scared even though there was nothing on the empty beach to fear. The long sand strip was backed by a low dune covered with tall grass—no houses, no people, not even a seagull.

Rachel dropped into the water and began swimming.

Carlos started up the engine and drove the boat onto the beach impatiently. "This good enough for you?" he asked Tina as the bow dug into the soft sand.

Tina was gripping the gunwales, staring behind her into the water. "There's stuff down there."

"Nothing that can hurt you. Get out," Carlos told her.

Cautiously Tina crawled over the bow and stretched a skinny leg onto the sand.

"The water's great, Carlos. Come for a swim before you start fishing," Rachel said.

"No. Later. After I catch enough."

Rachel walked up out of the water and heaved the picnic cooler and jug out of the boat onto the beach. "We should have brought towels," she said.

"It's warm enough to dry off in the sun," Carlos said. He put the engine in reverse, and the boat moved away, helped by a shove from Rachel.

He is one determined fisherman, Rachel thought respectfully.

In a couple of minutes Carlos was fifty feet from shore. He tossed out his anchor and began setting up Ben's rod.

"How many fish do you think he'll figure is enough to pay for his board and keep today?" Tina asked Rachel.

"That's what you think he's trying to do?"

"Oh yeah. Carlos is proud. He hated it that his father was sending him off to strangers like a charity case."

"I thought he just loved fishing," Rachel said.

Tina snorted.

"Do you want to eat a sandwich or drink something?" Rachel asked.

Tina was looking around uneasily. "How are we going to get out of the sun?" she wanted to know. "We're going to be cooked. There isn't even a tree or a bush or anything. It's just sand and more sand."

Rachel loved it that the beach was deserted and purely

natural, but she didn't argue. "Did you put sunscreen on this morning?" she asked Tina.

"I don't have any...I wish I'd brought my hat." She eyed the hat Rachel was wearing—Ben's hat—but Rachel didn't offer it to her. She reasoned to herself that Tina was olive skinned and couldn't burn as easily as Rachel would even with sunscreen.

"Too bad we didn't bring a tarp or something to build a shelter with," Rachel said. "I'll go look and see if there's anything in the dunes or on the other side of the beach we could use."

"Like what? Seashells?" Tina asked sarcastically.

"Like boards or plastic sheets. Stuff washes up on the beach."

"I'll go with you," Tina said as if she feared being left alone. She glanced out to where Carlos was still standing upright in the boat. He flicked his rod so that his line flew way out over the water before it sank. "I hope he catches something fast," she said.

The beach was clean even on the bay side of the dune. There no land broke the horizon line. A couple of plastic bottles and a tangled greenish rope knotted through a stick was their total find when Tina said, "I'm so thirsty. Let's go back, Rachel."

Aware suddenly of a change in light, Rachel noticed that the storm clouds that had been over the bay were advancing on them in an ominous mass. "Looks like we may not have to worry about sunburn anyway," Rachel said.

Sure enough, by the time they'd finished the lemonade—which Tina complained was too sweet—clouds had blocked the sun. Carlos seemed to have caught something. They saw him pulling a fish over the edge of the boat and whacking it with a rubber club.

"Carlos," Tina yelled, "let's go home now."

Either he didn't hear her or he pretended not to.

Chapter 10

RACHEL ATE A SANDWICH. They were going to get rained on, and Ben hadn't remembered to put slickers in the boat. At least she hadn't seen any.

Thunder cracked, startling Tina, who was picking up scallop shells and bringing them back to stow in the cooler with the lunch. "What's that?" Tina yelled. She dropped the shells and made a megaphone of her hands. "Hey, Carlos! Get in here now. We got to get back to the house."

"Yeah. In a minute. They're biting good." He was hauling in another fish.

Lightning flashed. The waves had picked up height and were peaked with whitecaps. The sea and sky roiled with menace.

"I don't like this," Tina said. "There's nothing here to get under. We're going to get killed."

"No, we're not. We can walk out of here if we have to," Rachel said. "But I think we're four or five miles from the National Seashore parking lot, and there's no houses or anything in between."

"Oh great. I never walked more than the length of a mall in my life."

"Anyway, we can't leave Carlos."

"Why not? He left us...Carlos!" Tina screamed. "Stop fishing and get your butt back here."

"Wait a minute!" he yelled. He was trying to subdue a fish, a big one. Not an easy task, Rachel knew. Bluefish died hard, no matter how vigorously they were bludgeoned.

Meanwhile more thunder rumbled and lightning zigzagged across the slate gray sky. The boat was rocking from side to side in the waves. And then the rain smacked them with the first cold drops.

Tina cursed. "I hate this place!" she cried. "I want to get *out* of here."

"Tina, don't be silly. It's just a little storm," Rachel said.

"You call him in then. See if he'll come for you."

"Carlos," Rachel yelled, "please, come back for us now."

He looked up, saw her, and reached for the anchor line. He pulled at it, but though he seemed to be putting all his muscle power into hauling up the anchor, nothing happened. Carlos tried again, and then again, but he couldn't budge the anchor. The boat was taking on water as it wallowed in the high waves. Carlos was in trouble. He stopped to bail a little and then tried starting the engine. A wave washed into the boat and Carlos, who was standing up to work on the engine, went backward into the bay.

Without any thought, Rachel ran to the water and dove in. She had no trouble swimming out to the boat because that was the way the strong current was taking her. When she reached it, Carlos was hanging on to the anchor line.

"I can't pull it up," he said.

Rachel grabbed the boat as it dipped sideways toward her on a wave and heaved herself into it. Then she scrambled to the opposite side to balance the craft as it lifted out of the water. The boat that had seemed so sturdy and safe in calm water now appeared flimsy in the angry waves. It was in danger of being swamped.

Carlos clambered back into the boat.

"I'll bail and you try to get the anchor up," Rachel said. "It must be stuck on something."

"I know," he said. "I'll try starting the engine again. If I could turn us around to pull from a different direction, maybe—"

Muttering in Spanish, he tried the engine, and when it wouldn't start he went back to hauling on the anchor line again. Rachel saw his arm muscles straining but the anchor didn't come up.

"Let me help," she said, and joined her weight to his on the line. The anchor was stuck fast.

Carlos went back to struggle with the engine. "I don't know why it won't start," he said. Meanwhile the white-tongued waves licked at them meanly and the boat pitched and yawed.

Out of the corner of her eye Rachel glimpsed Tina on shore. She was crouched into a tight little ball with her hands over her ears. No doubt she was screaming, but with the thunder and the wail of the wind Rachel couldn't hear her.

"Could be the condenser, a bad plug or something," Carlos said about the balky engine.

Rachel could barely hear him in the rush of wind and crackle of thunder. She was having trouble keeping her balance in the heaving boat, and with a quarter of it full of water, she was afraid it was going to sink. She let go of the line and emptied the bucket of fish he'd caught back into the harbor. She needed the bucket to bail with. Carlos wasn't showing any fear, just frustration at not being able to make that engine start. Rachel wasn't terrified either, anxious, but not terrified. They were close enough to shore that they could make it if they had to swim for it.

"Boy, I'm stupid. I'm so stupid. I can't do anything right," Carlos said.

"Maybe we're out of gas."

He looked around him wildly. "Where's the gas can?"

Rachel searched the water-filled boat with her eyes. "It's gone," she said.

Together they set to bailing. Rachel's shoulders ached, but the water kept coming in. The streaming rain was slowing now and as suddenly as they had come, the thunder and lightning passed. The rain stopped and everything grew quiet except for the slap of the four-foot waves against the boat. By the time the first finger of sun reached the gunmetal gray water, the waves were calmer and the whitecaps were gone.

"You might as well come back to shore," Tina called. "I'm not going in that boat and I can't walk out of here alone."

"The fish are gone," Carlos said sadly. "I had four big ones."

"I'm sorry," Rachel said. "I needed that bucket to bail with."

He shrugged. "It's OK," he said with resignation. Then he tried tugging on the anchor line again. It didn't budge.

"Carlos, we better leave the boat here. It's about a four- or five-mile hike to a parking lot where we might find someone to take us home," Rachel said.

"I'll stay with the boat," Carlos said.

"No, I don't think Ben would like that. We should stick together," Rachel said. "The boat's not going anywhere. Ben'll have to get a neighbor to come out here and help him rescue it."

Carlos shook his head. "So stupid. How could I be so stupid?"

"It wasn't your fault. It was the storm."

"I'm a fisherman. I know about storms. I know about boats. And look what I did!" He sounded agonized.

Tina said, "If you guys don't get back here, I'm going to start screaming and I won't stop." She gave them a sample of her screaming.

Carlos gritted his teeth.

"OK?" Rachel asked. "Shall we go?"

"OK," he said.

They dove over the side together and swam to shore.

Rachel persuaded Tina and Carlos to wait long enough to finish off the lunch. "Otherwise we've got to carry that cooler and it's heavy," she said. What she thought was that Carlos would feel better with some food in his stomach.

He ate mechanically, staring at the boat. He seemed depressed by his failure. Tina shivered and complained about not being hungry.

"I don't know if I can walk four miles. I don't know if I can walk three," she whined.

"Then stay here," Carlos snapped.

"I'm not staying here alone," Tina said. "You're the one got us in this mess, Carlos. You think you're such a big shot. Well, you're not."

He didn't answer her, but his eyes squinted painfully at the boat riding so low in the water that it looked like a sick whale.

The walk was interminable. Rachel had hiked out this far and back with her mother and Ben on a picnic last year, but the round trip hadn't seemed as arduous as this one-way trek following the comfortable sandy path through the pine barrens. It was her companions who made it seem so long. Carlos was silent and sullen. Tina kept fretting about her feet blistering and asking, "How much farther?" Over and over she assured them she'd never make it.

To Rachel's relief, there was a car with New York license plates in the parking lot. An elderly couple dressed in sensible hiking shorts and shoes were just getting out of it. When Rachel explained the predicament she and Carlos and Tina were in, the sturdy white-haired couple volunteered to drive them back to town. The woman even provided the quarter to make a phone call home, and she wouldn't let the man leave until Rachel signaled her that her father had answered the phone.

"Where are you?" Ben asked Rachel as the New York couple drove off. "We've been frantic."

Rachel told him briefly what had happened. "Is Mom all right?"

"Fine," Ben said. "The doctor wants her to stay in bed for a few days. He said the bleeding's probably not too dangerous to the baby, so long as it doesn't get any worse."

"Good," Rachel said. "Ben, Carlos feels bad about the boat."

"I wasn't planning to cream him."

"I know—but I mean, he feels really bad."

"OK, honey. I get you."

In fifteen minutes Ben was there with the car. He picked up the bedraggled threesome who were sitting side-by-side on a bench in front of the town hall. Tina took the front seat next to Ben and gave him a hug and a kiss. "Thanks for rescuing us. I thought I was going to die," she said dramatically.

"Yeah, well, when you can't swim—," Ben said.

"The waves got high fast," Carlos said.

"Yes. Now you see what I mean when I say the weather changes quickly around here," Ben said. They drove past the art galleries on Main Street to Route 6 and waited for the light.

"You know, I didn't expect you to take off for Jeremy Point by yourselves," Ben said. "Whose idea was that?"

"Nobody's," Rachel put in to block any criticism of

Carlos. "I mean, all you said was, 'Stay close to shore.' You didn't say which one."

Ben shook his head. "Sorry I didn't make myself clear. I meant the one you were starting from, of course. Well, we're lucky nothing happened to any of you."

"I was so scared," Tina said leaning against him.

"Were you, honey? I'm sorry," Ben said. He put an arm around her and hugged her close to him. "I apologize. I was so frazzled by MJ's problem that all I could think of was getting her to the doctor."

"It wasn't your fault," Rachel said. "I should have known better. I wasn't thinking."

Carlos said nothing. He hunkered into himself as if he had no connection to anyone else in the car.

"Well, anyway, it's over and you're all all right," Ben said.

"The boat," Carlos said.

"We'll get it back," Ben said. "I'll get one of my neighbors to help me."

Carlos didn't seem consoled. He went directly to his room when they got home. Tina went to the one she shared with Rachel. Rachel checked in with her mother who wanted to hear the whole story in detail.

It was so comfortable lying there on the king-sized bed on the puffy quilt beside her mother that Rachel felt more and more sleepy. By the time she'd finished her tale, she just had to close her eyes, and the next time she opened them it was suppertime.

Chapter 11

TINA'S MOTHER CALLED when the family was at the dinner table that night. Rachel and Carlos were so ravenous after their boating experience that they were both on their second bowls of chili. But Tina hadn't touched the chili and was picking at her salad as if she weren't very hungry.

Ben got the phone on the first ring. The instant he said, "Tina, it's for you," her face lit up.

"My mom?"

Ben nodded and Tina bolted for the phone, sending her fork clattering onto the floor.

"Mom, why didn't you call me?" she cried.

MJ and Ben exchanged pitying looks, but the next thing out of Tina's mouth was, "I nearly drowned today."

Ben's jaw dropped. "Did she?" he whispered to Rachel.

"She wasn't even near the water in the storm. She's really scared of water," Rachel said quietly.

"Yeah, I know," Ben said. "I was the one trying to teach her to swim."

"You what?" Tina screeched into the phone so that all of them at the table focused on her. "Sure, I'll ask him."

She pressed the phone to her chest, smiling all over her face, and asked, "Ben, could you drive me to the airport in Boston?"

"Now?"

"No, when Mom sends me a ticket to come to Vegas."

"Las Vegas?"

"Yeah, she and Carlos's dad just won a bundle there. But they're splitting up and Mom says she needs me."

"You mean, they're splitting up with each other?" Ben asked.

"You got it," Tina said snippily.

"Sure, I'll drive you to the airport," Ben said. Disappointment weighted his voice. He must have thought Tina was glad to be with him and was having a good time here, Rachel thought. She felt sorry for Ben. He'd only had his daughter a very short time.

That night in their bedroom Rachel sensed Tina's wakefulness. Boldly into the darkness Rachel asked, "Are you going to give me back my hat before you go?"

"I didn't take it."

"I never did anything to you, Tina."

"So?"

"So why did you take my hat?"

"What a nag you are. It's just a hat. Ben'll buy you another one. He'd buy you anything, I'm sure. He's nuts about you."

"No. You're his daughter."

"He doesn't know me. You're the one he knows. Anyway, you're the good girl. Besides, who could resist those big blue baby-doll eyes?"

Scorn dripped from every word, but Rachel didn't cringe. She thought she was beginning to understand.

Tina rolled over in bed. "Go to sleep," she said. "You've got it made and you're too dumb to know it."

A week passed and nothing much happened.

The neighbors drove Ben over to Jeremy Point in their Boston Whaler and helped him raise his half-sunk boat and release it from the rusty iron hulk the anchor had become embedded in. It turned out that Carlos had guessed right about the engine. It had a bad spark plug in the condenser. Once he had been proved right about that, Carlos seemed to shed some of his guilt for the boating disaster. At least he held his head higher.

Tina spent her time with MJ, doing her quilt and listening to music while MJ rested with her feet up as the doctor had recommended.

Afternoons when her mother was lying on the lounge chair out back, Rachel fixed iced tea the way MJ liked it with honey and lemon, and she seemed grateful.

"This is a switch, isn't it?" MJ asked ruefully. "I mean, you waiting on me."

"Want some zwieback biscuits to go with the tea?" Rachel asked.

"That would be nice, thanks," MJ said.

And Rachel ran to the kitchen and outside again to the patio. She didn't mind waiting on her mother; in fact she found a certain satisfaction in that she could do it well.

In the evenings, Rachel walked the beach to see the sunset, sometimes alone, sometimes with Ben and Carlos and Tina. She swam every day, alone or with Carlos, and read in the lounge chair outside under a borrowed floppy straw hat of her mother's. Ben worked on patching the roof. No airline ticket came for Tina and now it was Carlos's father who didn't call. Carlos grew gloomier day by day. He spent so many hours fishing from the break-water that he filled the freezer with bluefish.

"Enough already," Ben said. "That's more than we can eat all summer."

Carlos shrugged. "We could sell it."

"Maybe," Ben said. "And you could ask the neighbors if they want any. Or we could just give them a batch for helping me get the boat back."

Dutifully Carlos took some bluefish to the helpful neighbors, asking Rachel to go along to front for him because he claimed not to know what to say.

"Want me to ask around to see if anybody'll buy blue-fish from you?" Rachel asked him on the way back.

"No, that's OK."

He watched television when he wasn't fishing or swimming. What he didn't do was use the boat. He gave it a wide berth, and he didn't seem to want anything much to do with Ben either.

"He's sulking," MJ said. "I wonder why."

"I think he's feeling bad, not just because the boat sank but because his father hasn't called like he promised Ben he would," Rachel said.

"Oh that's ridiculous, Rachel. How could he blame himself for the storm or his father's behavior?"

"But he does." Rachel thought she understood Carlos even if Tina was beyond her.

"Did the mail come yet?" Tina asked every day.

The weather was beautiful, but even Rachel was having trouble keeping her spirits up in the dismal fog of Carlos's and Tina's moods.

A week and a half later the ticket to Vegas finally came.

Tina was so enthused about going off to her mother that she threw her arms around each of them in turn and kissed them good-bye. Carlos jumped back when she tried to kiss him, but Ben hugged her hard and long and told her he hoped she'd come back and visit them often.

"You come whenever you like and stay for as long as you like, sweetheart," he said. "Remember you're my girl, too."

When Tina offered to kiss *her* on the cheek, Rachel accepted in silence. She'd given up hoping Tina would relent and give her back the hat. Probably she couldn't return it, Rachel decided. Probably the hat had been destroyed.

Two days after Ben had driven off with Tina to the airport, a small thin man with high cheekbones and a beautiful head of hair appeared just as they were sitting down to dinner.

"Papa!" Carlos shouted. He jumped up and led his

father through the door that Ben had opened. "This is my father," he said to MJ. "Antonio Juan Frederico Sanchez."

Mr. Sanchez bowed. "Thank you for taking care of my son," he said. "I am here to pay you for his board and to take him home to Puerto Rico."

"We're going home?" It was Carlos's turn to radiate joy.

Rachel was taken anew by how handsome he was when he smiled. She hadn't seen his smile in days.

Ben and MJ insisted Mr. Sanchez sit down to dinner, and they asked him how he had managed to get to them. "Every which way," he said. "Sometimes I rode the bus, and sometimes people gave me rides, and sometimes I had to walk." He smiled as if it had been a fine adventure. "Tina's mother told me how to get here," he said.

"You walked and you hitched?" Ben asked. "But I thought you and Tina's mother won a pile of money."

"We did. We did for sure," Mr. Sanchez said happily. "But two plane tickets to Puerto Rico cost a lot. And of course, I can't return home without presents for my wife and children." Mr. Sanchez's smile was so irresistible they all returned it.

There was an argument after dinner about his payment for Carlos's board. Ben assured him that Carlos had caught enough fish to cover it. "Carlos is a fine boy. We were glad to have him," Ben said.

"Yes, Carlos is a very good boy," Mr. Sanchez said proudly. "He takes after my wife, and she is the best woman in Puerto Rico." He reached over and rubbed his hand over Carlos's curls affectionately.

"We thought you were involved with Tina's

mother," MJ said questioningly, as if Mr. Sanchez puzzled her.

"Oh, that one, yes." For the first time Mr. Sanchez looked embarrassed. "Sometimes you make a mistake, you know? Sometimes you go a little loco." He gestured to show them how crazy one could get, and then he shrugged and smiled again.

In the morning Ben drove Carlos and his father to where they could catch the bus to the airport. Rachel was sorry to see Carlos go even though he didn't seem to mind leaving. He shook MJ's hand and hers briefly and that was it. No words. Not even much expression on his face. It disappointed Rachel that he cared so little about them.

"So," her mother said, "are you going to be bored with just Ben and me now that those kids are gone?"

"No," Rachel said. "It was sort of interesting to have them around, but it was also sort of complicated and hard."

"Umm," MJ said. "I know what you mean."

That night Rachel opened the book on her night table to read and a paper dropped out.

"Dear Rachel, You are a strong and beautiful girl. I am yours. Love, Carlos," the note said.

Rachel burst into tears. She was filled with such bittersweet joy she could hardly bear it. Why hadn't he said anything to her while he was with her? She'd liked him, and now he was gone and she didn't even know where to send him a letter. She studied the short note helplessly. His handwriting was large and childish and solemn, a reflection of him. Well, it was something of him to keep, she told herself, something precious, and she slipped the note back into the book so that she could have the pleasure of rediscovering it in the morning.

She was eating a bowl of cereal the next day when MJ came out of her bedroom with the blue straw hat. "Look what I found in the back of my closet behind the shoe rack," MJ said. "I was looking for an old skirt with an expandable waistband and came upon this."

"*That's* where Tina must have hidden it," Rachel said. She took the hat, which seemed none the worse for wear, and put it on her head and smiled.

"She was jealous of me, Mother. You know that? Tina was actually jealous of *me*."

"Well, you've got a lot going for you, Rachel, and Tina has a lot of problems."

"I guess she does, doesn't she? . . . You know what?" Rachel said, taking her mother's hand into hers. "I've been thinking about it—I mean, about having a baby brother or sister—and I've decided I might like it."

"Oh, Rachel!" MJ hugged her. "I'm so glad."

Rachel was, too. For the first time since they'd come to Ben's cottage she felt good about herself. After all, she wouldn't stay a child forever. There were voyages ahead of her—things to do, places to see, and people to meet. Someday she might even take a trip to Puerto Rico and look up Carlos. And if Tina came back for a visit, well, she and Rachel each had her own hat now.